LIBRARY
ST. MARYS AREA MIDDLE SCHOOL
979 S. ST. MARYS ROAD
ST. MARYS, PA 15857

D1266733

The
Ghost Squad
and the
Ghoul of Grünberg

By the Same Author

GHOST SQUAD BOOKS

The Ghost Squad Breaks Through
The Ghost Squad Flies Concorde
The Ghost Squad and the Halloween Conspiracy

THE McGURK MYSTERIES

OTHER BOOKS

Manhattan Is Missing
Louie's Lot
Louie's Ransom
Time Explorers, Inc.

The Ghost Squad and the Ghoul of Grünberg

by E. W. Hildick

A Ghost Squad Book

E. P. DUTTON   NEW YORK

Copyright © 1986 by E. W. Hildick

All rights reserved. No part of this publication may be
reproduced or transmitted in any form or by any means,
electronic or mechanical, including photocopy, recording,
or any information storage and retrieval system now
known or to be invented, without permission in writing
from the publisher, except by a reviewer who wishes to
quote brief passages in connection with a review written
for inclusion in a magazine, newspaper, or broadcast.

LIBRARY OF CONGRESS CATALOGING IN PUBLICATION DATA

Hildick, E. W. (Edmund Wallace), date.
  The Ghost Squad and the Ghoul of Grünberg.

  (A Ghost Squad book)
  Summary: The crime-fighting Ghost Squad joins
forces with living colleagues to find out the fate
of a missing boy at a camp which seems to be headed
by a former commandant of a Nazi death camp.
  [1. Ghosts—Fiction.   2. Mystery and detective
stories] I. Title. II. Series: Hildick, E. W.
(Edmund Wallace), date. Ghost Squad book.
PZ7.H5463Ge 1986 [Fic] 85-29350
ISBN 0-525-44229-4

Published in the United States by E. P. Dutton,
2 Park Avenue, New York, N.Y. 10016,
a subsidiary of NAL Penguin Inc.

Published simultaneously in Canada by
Fitzhenry & Whiteside Limited, Toronto

Editor: Julie Amper

Printed in the U.S.A.   COBE   First Edition
10 9 8 7 6 5 4 3 2

Contents

1
The Shadow and the Shadowed

"They're here now!"

As the two newcomers appeared at the corner of the tree-lined street of big old houses, Carlos Gomez gave an impatient little leap and turned to his three companions. His eyes sparkled under the thatch of shaggy dark hair. Not for the first time, he reminded the tallest of the others of a young sheepdog, bristling with strange new skills that he could hardly wait to start using once again.

"OK, Carlos! Take it easy!" said the tall one—a husky red-haired young man dressed only in jeans and a T-shirt, despite the late November chill. "They won't go in without *us*."

As the young man was speaking, the newcomers advanced into the pool of light from a streetlamp. One was a thin, serious-faced, fifteen-year-old black kid, with his hands deep in the pockets of a heavy raincoat. The other was a broad-shouldered, carefree-looking white kid of about the same age.

The latter was doing most of the talking. The black kid didn't say anything. He just nodded and grunted from time to time, in a somewhat doubting manner.

They were still too far away for the waiting four to hear what was being said. But they were close enough to have seen the group, none of whom was making any attempt to hide in the shadows.

Yet the newcomers didn't show the slightest sign of recognition. Not even when Carlos yelled, "Come on! Let's get ready!" and started off up the driveway, only a couple of paces in front of the two boys.

The black kid seemed to see only a sudden swirl of dust and dry leaves.

"Snow," he grunted. "That's a sure sign of snow."

"Sure, but . . ."

His companion went on to finish what he was saying, but the others weren't listening any longer. Two of them—the tall one and a boy in a black imitation-leather windbreaker and red nylon scarf—had already started up the driveway, but the fourth member of the waiting group still lingered on the sidewalk.

"No! Wait!"

Her voice rang out, alerting her three companions immediately. But, as before, the other two paid no attention. The black kid was pressing the doorbell.

"What's wrong, Karen?" asked Carlos, from his perch on the doorstep.

"They—there's a man further along the street, and I think—"

2

"So what?" said Carlos. "He won't see *us!* . . . Anyway, here's Wacko's mom coming to open the door. Hurry up or you'll get left on the sidewalk."

But the girl didn't move. The fact that she was the flimsiest-dressed of them all—in white shorts and a thin sleeveless red shirt—didn't seem to make any difference. Being left out in the cold obviously didn't worry her at all. The sight of the man did, though.

"He's been following Buzz and Wacko. I could swear he has. He's stopped now, but—"

"You sure about this, Karen?"

The redheaded one was already back on the sidewalk; the boy in the windbreaker close behind. Even Carlos had started to move away from the door, which was just being opened.

"I'm sure, Joe," said Karen. "I saw him earlier, on Main. He'd been looking in the window of that radio-equipment store, and when Buzz and Wacko came out, he started walking along behind them."

"So why didn't you come and report it?" said Joe. "This could be serious!"

He was staring at the man, who'd stopped under the streetlamp and appeared to be puzzling over the address on an envelope. The man *seemed* respectable. Under his parka, open at the front, he had on a neat dark business suit. He was slightly built.

"I thought it was just a coincidence," said Karen.

Carlos glanced back up the driveway. The door was still open. Buzz and Wacko were still standing there, but Mrs. Williams had gone back into the house. Wacko was peering out nervously.

But Carlos himself was no longer eager to go inside. Not now.

"He doesn't seem to be coming any further," said Joe as the man glanced at the name on a nearby gate, then back at the envelope, then shrugged.

"He doesn't need to, does he?" said Karen. "Now that he's seen where Wacko lives."

"Shouldn't we go in while the door's open?" said the boy in the windbreaker. "So we can warn them and—huh!"

It was already too late. The door had been closed.

"No. We have to see what this guy does next," said Joe. "Follow *him*, if necessary."

The man advanced a few paces in their direction but stopped again. And again he peered at the envelope, checking whatever address was on it with the name at the entrance to the next house.

"Shouldn't we—?" Karen was distracted by a sudden change in the shadows. Up beyond the bare twigs of a maple tree, a window on the third floor of Wacko's house blazed out. Wacko's head and shoulders appeared as he started closing the drapes.

The man had been staring up at the window. But not for long. With another glance at the envelope, he turned and, shaking his head, began walking back in the other direction.

"Right!" said Joe. "Let's see where he goes next."

Joe made no attempt at stealthiness, no keeping close to the shadows. Only the boy in the windbreaker hesitated.

"Hey, Joe!" he whispered, plucking at the leader's

4

sleeve. "Watch it! Suppose—suppose he's like *us*—one of *us*?"

"Wow, yeah!" gasped Carlos, making a sudden neat side step closer to the bushes.

Joe didn't falter. Nor did he bother to keep his voice down.

"Would he need to use the envelope routine to quiet any passerby's suspicions if he *was* one of us? Would he be *able* to, even? Anyway, something tells me we'll soon find out."

The man had turned the corner. They followed him into another, similar street of big houses.

"He must have been keeping watch on the Phillips house," said Karen. "Then followed them from there."

Sure enough, the man crossed the street just before he reached Buzz's house and headed for a car parked alongside a vacant lot, about fifty feet farther on.

Then, as he unlocked the car door, opened it and stepped inside, Joe turned to the boy in the wind-breaker and said, "OK, Danny? *Now* are you satisfied he isn't one of us?"

The boy nodded. He looked relieved.

"Sure!"

Danny Green had been around in his present state for much less than a year. But he knew as well as the others that no ghost would ever have been able to open that car door.

2
The Ghost Riders

What ghosts *could* do, though, the four did next.

As the man started the engine, they clambered on board. Joe and Danny stood on the trunk, leaning over the roof, and Karen and Carlos took the hood, facing their friends. The fact that their living bodies would have obscured the driver's view, front and rear, made no difference now. As far as he was concerned, they just weren't there at all.

And so it was with the other living people around. No homegoing motorists found themselves swerving as they gaped at what could have been a very unnerving sight. No living pedestrian stopped to holler out a warning.

As the car moved off, they did pass a few pedestrians and motorists. But only two—both pedestrians—gave them so much as a casual glance. These were ghosts themselves. One was a man in pajamas and bathrobe, and the other was a woman in a light loose summer silk dress. Like all ghosts, these two were dressed in what they'd felt at their best or most comfortable in at the time of their deaths. A gust of wind did nothing to disturb the folds of the woman's dress—and that was another sign of ghosthood. And although the headlights swept across the man in the bathrobe as the car turned into Wacko's street, he cast no regular shadow. Just a vague gray shadow of a shadow that could be seen only by another ghost.

The car didn't go fast or far. If it had—if it had taken the bumpiest dirt road or gone 100 miles an hour—it wouldn't have given the four free riders the least trouble.

None would have been shaken off.

Karen's long blond hair wouldn't have been blown about—not unless she'd consciously wished and willed it to. Maybe if they'd had far to go, it might have made the others uneasy to see it behaving against all natural laws. Even ghosts can be made to feel spooked at times. In that case, Carlos might have said, "Hey, Karen! Let your hair blow, huh?"

The car came to a slow stop in the shadowy area between the Williams house and the next-door neighbors'. The lighted oblong of Wacko's window, now a rose pink because of the drapes, could still be seen through the bare branches and twigs overhead.

"*Now* what?" said Carlos, getting down.

"Maybe he's going to Wacko's house, after all," said Karen.

But the man made no move to get out. Instead he

switched on the interior lights and pulled out a street map, spreading it across his knees. Then he reached into a briefcase and took out a large notebook. They all bent forward to get a better look at the heading on the sheet he turned to.

"Hey!" said Carlos. "We've been wasting our time! He's just a sales rep, checking on his notes."

The heading seemed to say it all:

POLINSULATION, INC., White Plains, N.Y.

- Double glazing
- Aluminum siding
- Home and office insulation
- Solar heating

And underneath was a bunch of scribbled addresses, some ticked, some crossed out and some marked *Follow up w. phone call* or *Not in when visited*.

A couple of homegoing residents came past—a man and a woman. Had the driver been sitting in darkness, they might have hurried on, giving him a wide berth, maybe to phone the police department. But seeing him there, poring over his notes, disarmed them.

"Poor stiff!" said the man. "Probably hasn't booked a single new order all day, and he's wondering how to make his report look good."

"You think he's a salesman?"

"Sure of it! Poor stiff!"

The stranger did have that sort of look as he scratched his dark curly head and sighed. He had a round face with a mouth that looked quick to smile, even though he wasn't smiling now.

"There you are!" said Carlos. "Forget him and let's get ready to go in when Wacko opens the door again."

"Hold it!" said Joe. "This could be a blind."

"Yeah," said Danny. "And what's he doing *now?*"

The man had reached into the glove compartment and was taking out a small black instrument. It looked as if it might have been an electric shaver, until he unwound a cord from its base, with an earplug at the end.

"It's a portable tape recorder," said Carlos as the man put the plug in his ear. "A dictating machine. I tell you, he's just a salesman going over his notes."

"Maybe," murmured Joe. "But—"

The man had pressed a switch, but nothing seemed to be happening. He turned and wound down the window, partway. They heard him mutter in a faint foreign accent, "Stupid thing!"—as he fiddled with the earplug.

Then, with another sigh, he seemed to give up on it. He removed the plug, pulled another cord from the base of the instrument and fitted its end into a socket on the car radio. He pressed one of the buttons on the radio.

"Hold on!" drawled Carlos. "Now this *is* unusual!"

"What? The fact that—?"

Karen stopped. The hissing from the radio speakers had suddenly become less harsh, and they began to hear voices. Hastily, the man turned down the volume, but he still left the window open, and they could hear every word plainly.

And no—it *wasn't* notes being read out loud in a monologue.

This was a dialogue.

Nor was it a radio show.

The voices were unrehearsed and only too familiar.

They even seemed to address the eavesdroppers directly.

"Hey, you guys!" (And this was unmistakably Buzz speaking.) "Stop fooling around! We've something to tell you."

"I don't think they turned up at all," came Wacko's glum tones.

"Sure they did! We all agreed on 5:30. And now it's close to 5:45."

"They never play games like this. Not for this length of time. I'll go try again."

There was a faint sound of a door being opened. Then the hissing.

"Wow!" said Carlos. "He—he's bugged Wacko's room! That's a directional listening device, not a tape recorder. How in heck he planted the bug, I just don't—"

"Never mind that now," said Joe. "Wacko's obviously on his way to open the door. And this time we *do* go in!"

"But what about this guy?" said Danny.

"You and Karen stay here," said Joe. "Make sure you catch every word he overhears. And stay with him if he leaves before we return. . . . Carlos, come on! Quick! We have to warn them. This looks serious— very serious indeed!"

3
The Red Alert

They were only just in time.

Wacko was holding the door open, but his mother was already calling out to him from the kitchen.

"Henry, is that you again?"

"Yes, Mom." Wacko peered out into the driveway. "I thought I heard the doorbell."

"I didn't hear anything. *Is* anyone there?"

Wacko glanced back. His face relaxed when he saw that his mother hadn't come to investigate.

"No, I don't think so, Mom." His voice dropped to a whisper. "Hey, you guys—if you *are* there—make it snappy, huh?"

By now, Joe and Carlos had slipped through into the hall. Carlos touched Wacko on the top lip.

Wacko's face relaxed a little further.

"About time!" he whispered, closing the door. Then he felt gingerly at his lip. "Hey, but why the red alert?"

"Did you say something, Henry?"

Mrs. Williams poked her head around the kitchen door as her son and his invisible companions began to climb the stairs.

"No, Mom. Just thinking aloud."

Ghosts are invisible only to living persons. They can see each other, hear each other and feel each other. But they cannot make themselves heard by the living. And they can only just make themselves felt by the living, as Carlos and the other three had discovered. Whether they pressed hard, pinched or punched, it produced the same effect—a slight coolness, a faint brushing sensation, as of a tiny drop of rain in the wind or the touch of a fly.

Most people never gave this a second thought, even if they noticed it. Unless, like Wacko and Buzz, they had trained themselves to expect it and had even agreed on a Touch-Code with their invisible friends. In this group, a touch on the top lip meant red alert—a warning to be very careful.

Buzz Phillips was given one also, as soon as Carlos entered the room. Buzz had looked up on seeing Wacko at the door, and his mouth had opened. But the touch on his lip made him pause.

"Was that—?"

Again Carlos gave his lip a prod.

Buzz looked at Wacko. Wacko shrugged and turned to the long table, where he'd been sitting with his friend in front of a word processor. Its screen was blank but glowing a faint green.

Wacko moved his chair, widening the space between himself and Buzz. Both boys kept their eyes on the screen. Then Carlos stepped forward and hovered for a moment over the keyboard.

Standing back a little, Joe watched intently. It was always a strain, wondering whether Carlos would be able to perform yet again his miracle of controlled micro-micro-energy. True enough, Carlos knew the machine inside out, having worked on it with Wacko before his death, making modifications and adding refinements that only a kid of his electronic genius could even have dreamed of. But to be able to direct that ghostly energy so that it activated the keyboard, accurately, to communicate with the living—that was something else.

Joe—who was pretty good at focusing and directing his own micro-micro-energy in cruder forms—knew just how fiercely Carlos was having to concentrate. He found himself crossing his fingers, very tight, as Carlos did the opposite, spreading his fingers out and flexing them, and then—with a shake of the shoulders—starting to type in thin air, stabbing at the keys but never hitting them, always coming within a hair's breadth of making contact.

Suddenly, Joe breathed more easily.

The screen had begun to flicker. Words were beginning to appear.

"This is a warning! This is a warning! The room has been bugged. You have been followed. Someone is listening. Don't say—"

But already Buzz had turned.

"Hey! Is this a—?"

Joe had quickly stepped forward and rapped him twice on the top lip. Wacko gave a loud warning clearing of the throat and patted the casing of the screen.

The message there did the rest.

"Don't say anything out loud—anything that matters. Wacko, you type your remarks and queries. Buzz, use that notepad there. But don't—repeat do not—say anything important out loud. Especially about the Ghost Squad."

Carlos turned from the machine.

"OK, Joe?"

"You did just fine, Carlos. Now wait and let's see if the message has really gotten home to them. They look pretty stunned."

Buzz and Wacko did indeed look stunned. This was an emergency they'd never faced before. In the six months or so since Carlos had first made his breakthrough and they'd formed themselves into what Joe had called the Ghost Squad—combining to fight any crime the ghosts were able to get wind of—all communications here, in their headquarters, had been conducted in the same way. By the ghosts speaking through Carlos and the word processor, and Buzz and Wacko simply saying out loud whatever they had to say.

But it didn't take the boys long to recover. Buzz reached out for the notepad. Wacko very slowly and deliberately moved in front of the keyboard, giving Carlos plenty of time to step back—knowing how unpleasant it was for a ghost if a living person blundered into him.

Wacko tapped out just one word.

"Who?"

Carlos stepped back to his original position.

"*Don't know. Short dark-haired guy, pretends to be a sales rep. Aluminum siding and stuff. He's out there now, in a car. Listening to every word in this room. Or hoping to. Karen and Danny are with him.*"

"Hold it, Carlos," said Joe.

Buzz was scribbling on the pad. Carlos and Joe leaned over to see what the message was.

OK. Buzz had written. *Message received and understood. But we have to say something!*

As Buzz turned to the screen for a reply, Carlos said, "He's right, Joe. What shall I tell him?"

"This."

And, at Joe's dictation, Carlos's busy fingers transmitted the message: "*Agreed. But whatever you say, make it harmless. Pretend you're waiting for someone to get in touch with you over the radio. Like you were CB buffs. That should jibe with what the guy's managed to pick up already.*"

So a doubly strange dialogue took place up in Wacko's room, that evening. Out loud, as casually as they could make it appear, Buzz and Wacko said things like:

"Maybe they're using another frequency."

"Yeah . . . maybe. We could try the one they used before."

"OK . . . Just be quiet. I'm getting an awful lot of interference."

"Sunspots again?"

"Mmm yeah . . . Some kind of magnetic storm, anyway."

But the real conversation was silent, urgent, conducted through the screen and on the notepad.

Largely, it was in the form of an interrogation.

Carlos was still mystified about how the stranger had managed to plant a bug in that room.

"Has anyone been talking to you? Any stranger?"

The boys shook their heads.

"Did you notice anyone following you? Like some stranger you recollect seeing more than once, during the day?"

Buzz and Wacko frowned, trying to remember. But they ended by shaking their heads again.

"Think!" Carlos was getting rattled. *"Do you go around with your eyes closed? I mean—how about this afternoon, after you left the radio store?"*

Wacko slowly moved to the keyboard again.

"Sorry, but we just didn't suspect anything. I mean, why should anyone want to follow us? And if you don't expect it, you don't keep looking over your shoulder, right?"

Carlos's reply came flickering back as Wacko resumed his seat.

"OK, OK! But from now on, you'd better keep looking over your shoulder, buddy!"

"Cool it, Carlos!" murmured Joe. "Ask if anyone bumped into either of them."

"Huh?"

"Collided with them. Like a pickpocket in reverse. To plant a bug on them."

"Oh—yeah—sure . . ."

Carlos asked the boys that question and wasn't content with more headshaking for an answer.

"We're dealing with an expert here, dummies! He could have planted something on you just by brushing past you. Get up and search your pockets. Now!"

Looking rather abashed, Buzz and Wacko did as they were commanded. They found nothing.

"How about the soles of your shoes?"

"Soles of their shoes?" said Joe.

Carlos almost snarled his reply, so miffed was he at being baffled by the bug.

"It could have been planted in some bubble gum. Left on the doorstep. Just leave this to me, Joe, huh?"

But again he had no luck. As the boys looked at the screen, after dutifully inspecting their shoes, but mystified by the request, Carlos surged ahead with his interrogation.

"OK. So did anyone—anyone at all—give you anything? Like a pen, say? Or some publicity handout?"

They shook their heads.

"Well, how about visitors to the house, Wacko? Any telephone repairmen? Or someone checking for double glazing, insulation?"

"I doubt it," Wacko replied. *"Mom's pretty strict about letting people like that into the house. Not unless she's checked their ID's. And even if they did check out, she'd never let them out of her sight for one second. But I'll ask her."*

"Good," said Joe. "Tell him to do that. But later. Right now, tell them we'd better get back to Karen and Danny. Meanwhile, remind them to be very careful. And to be ready for an urgent meeting at any time. Tell them we'll be trying to find out what we can about the guy."

While Carlos was conveying all that, the boys nodded gravely.

"Buzz has arranged to come again, after dinner," Wacko typed. *"Suppose we make it eight o'clock. Do you think you'll have something more to report by then?"*

"*We should have,*" came the reply. "*Expect us then, anyway.*"

Wacko nodded and typed: "*Will do.*"

Joe was just preparing to leave when he remembered something else.

"By the way, ask them what they meant—when we heard them over the guy's listening device—saying something about something they had to tell us."

Carlos passed this query on, and, grinning rather bashfully, Wacko took over the keyboard.

"*Oh,* that! *I guess it wasn't so special. Just some record material. Something we put on the machine's memory. About the personnel of the Ghost Squad.*"

"About *what?*" yelled Joe. "Hey, Carlos—you'd better find out about *that!*"

To Carlos's request for further details, Wacko replied by pressing a button on the keyboard and bringing up on the screen, ready processed, the following data:

Personnel—The Ghost Squad

JOE ARMSTRONG
Age at time of death: 23

Former occupation: Head of own construction company (youngest in the business)

Cause of death: Fall from tenth story of building under construction. Believed by Joe to be murder, having been pushed by person unknown.

18

The words ARMSTRONG CONSTRUCTION, stenciled on the front of Joe's T-shirt, began to rise and fall. But it was not with pride. His lips got tighter and tighter as his own details were followed on the screen by those of the others:

Of Karen Hansen, whose age at the time of death (and therefore for as long as she stayed around as a ghost) was given as sixteen, and whose cause of death was listed as "run over by a truck";

Of Danny Green, fourteen, who'd been buried under tons of bricks and rubble while exploring an old factory;

Of Carlos Gomez, thirteen, who'd accidentally been electrocuted while "working on an experimental word processor at the home of his friend, Henry 'Wacko' Williams."

"The dumb jerks!" Joe exploded. "Look at them! Proud of it! Tell 'em to wipe it all off! Erase it! Immediately! Now!"

Carlos had never seen Joe look so mad.

"But—"

"Don't *you* be so stupid, Carlos! Think! Think of what might happen if the guy down there had some kind of *visual* snooping device. Or the place was burglarized. Or even if Wacko's mother or father happened to see what was on there."

"Gosh! You're right!"

Carlos lost no time in transmitting the order, and it was a very shamefaced Wacko who let him out at the front door, a few minutes later.

"Not *again!*" they heard Mrs. Williams say as they went down the driveway.

"Poor old Wacko!" murmured Carlos, grinning. "This just doesn't seem to be his day, does—?"

His companion had gripped his arm. They had reached the sidewalk, and Joe was staring at the car.

There were now three figures bending over the door. The new one was a tall well-dressed man who was saying something through the open window.

"Hey! Isn't that Mr. Williams?" said Joe.

"Yes, but—what's he doing? He seems quite friendly. Don't tell me *he's* in on this bugging thing!"

Mr. Williams was taking a small slip of white paper or card from the driver.

"Thanks," they heard him say. "I'll bear it in mind."

Then he put it in his pocket and moved away, almost walking right through the astonished Carlos who sidestepped only just in time.

4
Camp Wednesday

"What was that all about?" asked Joe, when they reached the car.

"It was—"

"Sorry, Karen," said Joe, interrupting her. The man was starting the engine. "But get on board. All of you. We just have to stick with him until we find out who he really is, and what he's really doing. You can tell us about Mr. Williams on the way."

They took up their earlier positions, with Joe and Danny on the trunk and Karen and Carlos on the hood—leaning over the roof so that their heads came close together.

The car began to move off.

"On the way *where*, though?" said Danny.

"We'll soon find out," said Joe.

For the first few minutes, the car went fairly slowly, down into the center of town. Then, rather more confidently, the driver went through the residential area to the south.

"This is the route to the Lakeview Hotel," said Karen. "Wouldn't it be funny if he's staying where Jackman stayed?"

Nobody spoke for a few moments. The Jackman case had been one of their major triumphs, back in July. Not only had the Ghost Squad taken a trip to London to track down a murderer but, in the process, they had also managed to foil a terrorist bomb plot.

"Not really," said Joe. "After all, the Lakeview Hotel is one of the few places he *could* be staying. Anyway, this might not turn out to be another crime. There may be some innocent explanation for his behavior."

They were now in a more open, rural area, and ahead of them, glittering and glimmering from a darker wooded patch, they could already see the colored lights festooning the hotel's parking lot.

But although the car did slow down there, it went straight past the entrance and began picking up speed again.

"Could be he's leaving the area altogether," said Danny. "Heading for New York. Maybe White Plains. He *could* be a genuine rep for that insulation firm, I guess."

Carlos grunted.

"Huh! Using sophisticated bugging equipment? *Super*sophisticated bugging equipment? Anyway, what did happen with Mr. Williams?"

"That's what makes me think he might be genuine," said Danny.

"Oh?" Joe looked at him.

"Yes," said Karen. "I'm inclined to agree with Danny. I mean, when Mr. Williams came along, obviously staring at the car, the guy didn't switch the interior light off or prepare to move away."

"How about the radio, though?" said Carlos.

"Well, yes," said Karen. "He did turn that off."

"I'll just bet he did!" said Carlos.

But Joe was frowning.

"What had he heard before Mr. Williams arrived?"

"Nothing much," said Karen. "We heard Buzz start to say something, then break off. So we guessed you'd given him a warning. Right, Danny?"

"Yeah," said Danny. "Then silence, and to me, anyway, it sounded real suspicious. It had the guy turning up the volume and fiddling around with the thing, turning it this way and that."

"But then Buzz and Wacko started coming through clearly again," said Karen. "Talking about radio interference."

"Like *they* were fiddling around," said Danny. "Trying to pick up some radio signal."

"And that seemed to make the man more relaxed," said Karen.

"You think he bought it, though?" Joe was still frowning anxiously.

"It's hard to say," said Karen. "Anyway, that's when Mr. Williams showed up."

The car was now climbing into a gently undulating countryside of farmsteads and woods. It was still familiar territory to the ghosts, no more than five or six miles from the center of town.

"Yeah," said Joe. "Mr. Williams. Tell us more about that."

"Well, I guess Mr. Williams thought it looked suspicious," said Danny. "You know—a car parked near his house like that, after dark. And him being a lawyer and all."

Carlos nodded.

"You bet! Especially a lawyer with the state's attorney's department. More like cops, some of those guys. Did he ask the guy straight out what he was doing there?"

Karen smiled.

"He was much more subtle and polite than *that!* He asked the man if he could be of any help. Like maybe he thought he was lost or something."

"And how did the guy react?" asked Joe.

"Totally relaxed," said Karen. "He said no—he was just covering the area for his firm and that it was new territory. He said he was just going over his notes while they were fresh in his mind. Ready for tomorrow's visits."

"Did he say which firm he was with?" asked Carlos.

"Sure," said Danny. "The one on the notepad. He even gave Mr. Williams his calling card and asked if *he* might be interested." Danny grinned. "He said some of those big old houses looked like they could use some extra insulation!"

Joe's face remained serious.

"And what did Mr. Williams say?"

"He said he'd think about it," said Karen. "That's when you arrived."

Carlos looked relieved.

24

"Yeah—that's what he *said!* But I bet Mr. Williams checks up. I bet he's called that firm already."

"Well—whatever," said Danny. "I still say the guy didn't seem worried. He—"

The car was slowing down. They'd just taken a sharp bend, on a rise, but instead of going on to the next bend, the car turned in at a gate. The gate was open, and it seemed to lead to nothing but a field track, but, arching over the gate, picked out by the car's headlights now, was the somewhat weatherbeaten sign: CAMP WEDNESDAY.

"Now why would he be coming *here?*" murmured Joe as the car passed under the sign, slowly, lurching on the bumpy track. "At *this* time of the day?"

"At this time of the *year!*" said Carlos.

The name was familiar to them all. Camp Wednesday was a summer camp—a very expensive one—that attracted older students from all over the country. Especially boys between the ages of fourteen and eighteen who were keen on electronic science.

"I once came here with Wacko on one of their At-Home Days," said Carlos as, still very slowly, the car made its way between overgrown fields. The long dry coarse grass, gray in the lights of the car, stirred uneasily in the cold wind. "Don't let these weeds fool you. Wait until we reach the inner boundary. It—"

"Later, Carlos," said Joe. "The way the guy's driving now, he's obviously not as familiar with the layout as you are. I mean, if anyone can be said to drive furtively, that's what he's doing now. . . . And I'm wondering why."

Dried milkweed pods rattled secretively on either side

of them. The ghostly shape of a deer crossed the track ahead, paused, then went bounding into the weeds, white tail flashing, uphill toward a dark mass of trees through which the lights of a house could just be seen. On their left, the ground fell away to another mass of trees and the thin splashing sound of a stream.

"Yeah," murmured Carlos. "And I'm wondering just what link there is in this guy's mind between Buzz and Wacko and Camp Wednesday. It couldn't be because Wacko and I once visited the place for a few hours, nearly eighteen months ago, could it?"

"You'd better tell us about that visit, Carlos, after all," said Joe.

But now it was Carlos's turn to say, "Later."

They had just arrived at the inner boundary of Camp Wednesday—where there was another open gate and another sign. But this gate was painted a slick glossy white, and the sign was equally spick-and-span, with large gleaming gold leaf letters on a black background:

CAMP WEDNESDAY
"SCIENCE & SURVIVAL"
FOUNDER AND DIRECTOR: DR. HELMUT MENDELSSOHN

Below it was a strip of wood, painted white, with the words, in bold red letters:

POSITIVELY NO VISITORS
WITHOUT APPOINTMENT

"Warm and welcoming!" murmured Karen, dryly. "I wonder how our friend will respond to *that?*"

5
Dr. Mendelssohn at Work

The dimmed headlights now showed the uninvited visitors that the weeds and bumpy dirt road had given way to close-cut lawns and smooth blacktop. A white flagpole rose up directly ahead, its lanyards rattling. At its foot was a large direction board, indicating that the Staff Parking Lot and the Director's Residence lay to their right, the Computer Shops and RT Labs were half-right, the Administration Building, the Cafeteria and the Visitors' Parking Lot were straight forward, and the Theater, Gymnasium, Sports Facilities and Campers' Quarters were to the left.

Some of the main buildings loomed out of the darkness. There was a faint source of light, somewhere ahead, in what was probably the administration building, as well as brighter gleams from the house in the trees, up on the hill to the right. But the driver seemed to ignore these. Instead of making for the visitors' parking lot, he began what was to be a slow clockwise tour, going between what had to be the theater and the gym.

"Very fine-looking buildings," said Karen. "Not like the shacks at the camp *I* used to go to."

"A whole bunch of money's been spent *here*," murmured Joe, casting a professional eye on the theater.

"That's what I was saying," said Carlos. "You should see it in daylight, though. When the camp's in session."

They were passing a complex of tennis courts now, at the bottom of the slope. In front of them lay a darkened sheet of water, glowing a dull silver.

"That's the lake," said Carlos. "They were swimming in there, the day we visited. It's bigger than it looks in this light. Stretches way, way back."

"What's that dark shape?" said Danny. "Some kinda tower?"

He was pointing to a black mass that rose out of the lake, a few hundred feet from the shore.

"That's a statue, on an island. It had only just been unveiled a couple of weeks before the At-Home Day."

"It looks huge," said Karen. "What's it a statue of? King Kong and his brother? I can just make out two heads."

"No. A couple of young guys, holding sextants and scrolls and stuff and gazing up at the sky. It's called *Art, Science and Youth*. There's a plaque somewhere along the edge of the lake."

The car was moving away from the water now, climbing again.

"I remember it caused a whole heap of construction problems," said Joe, glancing back at the towering

28

mass. "Mainly with the concrete foundation. I heard Angus MacGregor, the guy who won the contract, grumbling about it one day. I forget the details but—boy—was he steamed up!"

The road had narrowed and was winding in and out, among bushes and long low cabins with cedarwood sides and jutting air-conditioners.

"Are these the campers' quarters?" said Karen, goggling.

"Sure are!" said Carlos.

"Wow! Those guys must really be spoiled rotten!"

"Don't let it fool you. From what we heard that day, the poor jerks had to rough it as well."

"Yeah?" murmured Joe. "Tell us more about that visit, Carlos. You say you came with Wacko?"

"Yes," said Carlos. "Back in July last year. Not long before I—uh—got transferred to another plane." He sighed. "Well, anyway—we'd no idea *that* was going to happen, and Wacko and I were thinking we might enroll the following year. They specialize in electronics, you know."

"That would be the science part," said Karen, thinking about the sign. "But what about—?"

"Anyway," said Carlos, "we weren't here for more than half an hour before we started getting messages."

"Messages?" said Joe.

"Yeah! That blacks and Hispanics weren't especially welcome."

"But that's discrimination!" said Karen. "Couldn't you have reported them? How about Wacko's father? Couldn't *he* have—"

"They weren't all that keen on girls, either," said Carlos, with a wry grin. "But no. It wasn't the people running the camp so much as the students themselves. A real snide bunch, most of them." He shrugged. "Besides, they also run a pretty tough course in physical fitness and what they called survival techniques."

"That's what I was about to ask you," said Karen. "Science and Survival."

"Yeah, well. Long hikes with only a few lousy biscuits to keep you going. Swimming with heavy packs on your back—supposed to be field transmitters that you couldn't get wet. Endurance tests. I tell you. That just wasn't Wacko's scene at all." He grinned again. "Not mine, either—in fact!"

They were near the top of the incline now, where the ground flattened out to form a sort of plateau before rising again into the trees.

"I'd like to take another look in *there*," Carlos said as they drove, even more slowly, past a large two-story brick building. "That's what they call the RT labs—but there's much more than ordinary radio transmission work going on in *there*, believe me!"

The car kept going, past another similar building.

"And in there," said Carlos, wistfully, "that's where the computer shops are. I'd have endured a few overnight hikes to have spent a summer there."

"And being discriminated against?" said Karen. "Would you have endured that?"

Carlos's eyes flashed.

"No way!"

By now they were nosing along the side of the administration building. Through tall glass doors and windows, they could see rows of tables and neatly stacked chairs. A faint light shone through, from the far side.

"Cafeteria," said Carlos. "It joins onto the offices. The light must be coming from one of them."

The car came to a stop in the visitors' parking lot. There was no other car there. The driver got out and gazed around. He was carrying the briefcase under his arm. He seemed very relaxed.

"I wonder if he *does* have an appointment, after all?" said Joe as they began to follow him to the far corner, away from the cafeteria and toward the source of light.

Of the row of windows along the other side of the building, only two were lit up. A fainter light came from the glass panels of the door at the side of them— a door marked DIRECTOR'S OFFICE.

They peered inside through one of the windows while the man peered through the other. They saw a long well-furnished office with two desks. The desk nearer the door was unoccupied, with a shrouded typewriter on it. At the other desk, separated from the first by a waist-high planter filled with tall flowerless plants, a man sat bending over some papers. He was fairly small and plump, with a bald head and neat gold-rimmed glasses. He was wearing a white shirt and dark tie.

"I wonder if that's Dr. What'sisname himself?" said Danny.

"Mendelssohn," said Karen, giving it a rich German pronunciation. "The name is Mendelssohn. That's easy enough, isn't it?"

Joe smiled. Karen was proud of her German, he remembered. Her grandmother had come from Frankfurt. Karen once told him that she'd spent hours as a little kid, trying to teach the old lady English. "With the result," Karen had confessed, "that she still knew only a couple of dozen words, while *I* was quite fluent in German!"

Then Joe's smile faded. The stranger was rapping the door.

The man at the desk gave a slight start and looked up sharply. At the same time, he seemed to press a button under the edge of the desk.

Nothing happened for at least three seconds. Then suddenly the whole side of the building became flooded with light.

By now, the man inside had reached the door and was looking out, with an expression of mild interest. He opened the inner door but left the glass storm door shut. The visitor made no move to open it, but just stood there, clutching his briefcase and smiling nervously.

"Who are you?"

The other man's voice came through the glass—quite crisply but calmly.

"Uh—excuse me—but—"

"Speak up, please!"

"I—uh—excuse me, sir. I saw the light and—uh— have I the pleasure of addressing Dr. Mendelssohn?"

The other bowed his head very slightly. "Wait there, please," he said. "I was just about to leave."

They watched as he went to a stand and took down a short plain gray jacket with a fur collar. He put this on carefully, even fussily, smoothing down the folds—then took a neat fur hat from the rack.

"*He* doesn't intend to catch a cold," said Karen.

"No," Joe murmured. "Or anything else that might—"

He broke off.

There was the sound of footsteps from the corner. Also the rattle of a chain and a harsh rasping.

Then they appeared. The man and the dog.

The dog was a big black Doberman pinscher, straining at the leash, fangs flashing. The man, too, gave a strong impression of fangs. This was because of his crooked jutting front teeth—and *they* weren't bared in a smile of welcome, either.

The two newcomers approached, unhurriedly but steadily.

6
Wolfgang Makes a Statement

"Ah, Wolfgang!" said the doctor, his voice lilting slightly as he shut the door and stepped out under the lights. "We have an unexpected visitor."

The man with the dog didn't reply. He was staring at the visitor with cold half-closed eyes. He seemed to be about the same age as Dr. Mendelssohn and not much taller. But Wolfgang was leaner, lithe, moving like a man twenty or thirty years younger. His hair was iron gray, cut fairly short. He too wore a thick jacket, but there was no fur around *his* collar. His shirt was open, and his neck was weatherbeaten and sinewy. The crooked jutting teeth looked strong.

He stopped a few yards from the group. The dog tugged forward, growling softly, its eyes on the visitor. Wolfgang gave one sharp tug, and it came to a halt, but without stopping its growling or taking its eyes off the nervously smiling man.

"I'm glad it isn't one of those animals that are able

to see ghosts," said Karen. "I know it wouldn't be able to *do* anything to us, but—"

"Quiet, Prinz!" said Wolfgang, softly. "Sit!"

The dog immediately sat, but still without taking its eyes off the visitor.

"I didn't catch your name, sir," said the doctor.

The stranger, rather reluctantly, turned his back on the dog and faced Dr. Mendelssohn.

"No—I—uh—I am so sorry. My name is Mishcon. But here—here's my card."

Mendelssohn took it with a quizzical smile, showing a few gold fillings.

"Aluminum siding, Mr. Mishcon?" The smile broadened as he glanced up. "What makes you think we need that here? And why did you not call first?"

The visitor was smiling back. It was an apologetic smile.

"I—I'm sorry, doctor. It was on—uh—the spur of the moment. I was passing, and I saw the sign. I'd heard of your camp, of course—who hasn't? And when I saw that it fell within my new territory—well"—he shrugged—"I just couldn't resist the impulse."

"Really?" The eyes behind the gold-rimmed glasses had a mocking glint. "I still don't see why you should think we are likely customers for aluminum siding. Or—uh—insulation." He waved the card vaguely and gracefully. "As you can see, our buildings are very modern. And always in excellent repair."

He spoke with a much slighter accent than the visitor's. The latter's *w*'s came out strongly as *v*'s, but Dr. Mendelssohn's were almost like faint *f*'s.

"Well, no—of course!" said the stranger. "But we

35

have this new line—solar energy panels, plus a complete conversion system. It could save thousands of dollars. *Many* thousands of dollars in a place this big."

The doctor smiled.

"Ah, now *that* we would be interested in! But"—the smile was snapped off—"when we have had the opportunity to study your—uh"—another glance at the card—"Polinsulation's literature. Not before."

"But of course! Maybe you'd like our brochure." The man began to open the briefcase. Wolfgang took a step forward. The dog stood up and growled, straining at the chain. The visitor froze for an instant, then, much more slowly, reached into the case and pulled out a booklet.

Mendelssohn took it.

"Yes. Well. Perhaps I could give you a call," he said.

"Of course. I'll be staying at the Lakeview Hotel for a week or so. . . ."

As the stranger fastened his case, Wolfgang, behind him, bent to the dog and said something in German, in a quiet but clear tone.

Karen gasped and spun around.

"What's wrong?" said Joe.

"I—" She was staring toward the corner. Then she blinked, looked hard at Wolfgang, who was quietly patting the dog, and said: "Well! What a strange thing to say!"

"What?" said Joe. "What *did* he say?"

"He said, 'Excuse me, Mister Traveling Salesman, but your car has just caught fire!' "

The others turned. There was no sign of flames or smoke beyond the corner.

"Are you sure he said that?" asked Carlos.

"Absolutely!"

"Well, it didn't shock *our* guy," said Danny.

"No. Obviously *he* doesn't speak German, either," said Karen.

The man hadn't even turned his head. He was thanking Dr. Mendelssohn and apologizing once more for the interruption.

"We will be in touch," said the camp director, genially. "Wolfgang, please make sure that Mr. Mishcon can find his way out. This place is *such* a labyrinth in the dark."

There could be no mistaking the irony. The floodlights around the administration building were still on, and in their glare, even across at the other side of the parking lot, the flagpole stood out sharply, lanyards and all. So did the gate—very white, very clear—and very closed.

Karen caught her breath.

Danny said, "The guy with the dog must have closed it."

"Sneaky!" drawled Carlos.

"Yes, but he's opening it again now," said Joe, motioning for them to clamber aboard the car.

As they passed through, into the wilderness of weeds and potholes, Wolfgang stood erect, the dog by his side, and gave the driver a mockingly exaggerated salute. Coming from anyone else, it might have been an acceptable joke. But his face was immobile, the thin lips and crooked teeth frozen in a lopsided sneer.

It was the eyes, though, that impressed them the most—cold and hard and exceedingly watchful.

7
The Stranger's Revenge

Approaching the Lakeview Hotel, the driver again slowed down. But again he went past.

This time, however, it was for only a few hundred feet. Then he pulled in at a gas station, got out and made for the pay phone.

"*Now* we might find out something about him," said Joe.

The stranger no longer looked like the nervous apologetic person he'd been at Camp Wednesday. Now he moved purposefully. The smile had gone, and there was a different look in his eyes—hard and watchful as Wolfgang's. His glances swept the whole of the gas station's front area. Only when he was satisfied that there was no risk of being overheard did he start dialing.

Even then, he took extraordinary visual precautions. He hunched over the telephone, so that Carlos, who'd been hoping to put his prodigious memory for figures to work, was unable to get a good enough look at the number he was dialing.

"This is one very cagey guy!" he grumbled.

"Hi! Larry?" said the man, with another swift glance over his shoulder. "Gideon here. . . . No. Pay Phone. Gas station. Don't worry about *my* precautions. I'm only sorry you never learned our true language. It would have been an extra safeguard. . . ."

So began the one-sided conversation that the ghosts were able to describe laughingly, later, as The Stranger's Revenge. For it was impossible to hear anything of the other person, so firmly jammed against his ear did the man who called himself Gideon keep the receiver. Also he spoke in such a low tone that it was difficult to make out everything that was being said even at their end.

"It's almost as bad for us as it must have been for him, trying to guess what Wacko and Buzz were saying," murmured Carlos, during the first pause, while Gideon was listening to the other person.

"I wonder what language he meant?" said Karen. "It certainly couldn't have been—"

Joe hushed her. Gideon was speaking again.

"Yes. I've just come back from there. A preliminary scouting. . . . No. That is something I can't quite understand. They must have some very expensive equipment in those laboratories and workshops. And I'm quite sure they have some good security-alarm system. But there isn't the general overall tightness I'd have expected if they were involved in something very big. . . .

"Well, for instance, the gates were wide open. And

I was able to spend fifteen minutes cruising around without any challenge. Now, maybe I was being monitored, maybe not. I have a feeling I might well have been."

Carlos grinned and started to say something, but Joe shook his head. The man was continuing:

"But there was nothing so sensitive that they felt urged to take me out at the soonest possible moment. . . ." He paused, listening. Then: "Yes, sure! But that would figure. For all they knew, I might have been from some government agency—*this* government, I mean. And it would be very foolish of them to take out one of *those* fellows, merely on suspicion. Then they *would* be in trouble, and our work would be done for us. . . . Yes. So they played it very low key. . . .

"Oh, yes! I was able to take a very good look at him. At least the one *calling* himself Mendelssohn. And there again—well—I am not sure. He's the right age, and a person's looks can change a lot in forty years, especially with surgery. But—I don't know. He's either mellowed a great deal, or he is a brilliant actor. The other man, now—he does look like what he might have been. Some kind of mean NCO type—with a strong streak of barrack-room cunning. . . ."

"Wolfgang?" Danny mouthed. Joe nodded.

"Yes," continued the man. "*Extremely* cunning. He tried out a very neat little verbal trap behind my back"—(Here Karen caught her breath.)—"which didn't quite come off. I'll tell you about it some other time. But it told me that they are *very* sensitive to the possibility of *European* investigators sniffing around. Especially those with German backgrounds."

"Well!" murmured Karen. "How about *that*? *I'd* never have been able to resist turning around!"

"Anyway," the man went on, "the visit was a carefully calculated risk on my part. Because, whatever they suspected or didn't suspect, it's good to get them feeling uneasy. Maybe they'll make more mistakes, that way. Meanwhile, about the two boys. . . ."

The listeners bunched even closer to the man.

"Yes, well, I now have no doubts whatever about the Phillips boy. Positively he *was* the one who made that Tel Aviv bomb call." (Danny gasped. All of them looked shocked.) "How he got wind of the plot is still a mystery, but you were right in your hunch, I think. . . . Yes. Some kind of very sensitive monitoring equipment."

"He can say *that* again!" breathed Carlos.

"Yes. It was probably accidental. But whether the message they stumbled across came out of Camp Wednesday or from some other source is a different matter. I'm hoping to talk with them directly about it quite soon."

A convulsive ripple of consternation ran among the listeners. It must have caused a similar reaction at the other end, because Gideon went on to say, "But what else *can* I do? Obviously they're sympathetic. Otherwise why would they have passed on the warning? . . . No. Of course I won't tell them too much! No more than I have to, anyway. . . ."

In this pause, Joe said, "We're going to have to be

present at that meeting. Because *they* had better not tell *him* more than they have to, either!"

"Yes, it worked pretty well," Gideon continued. "But again—well—I had the distinct feeling they were being *deliberately* uncommunicative. As if they knew they were being overheard. Especially at the Williams house. . . ."

"You can bet on *that*, mister!" said Carlos.

"Maybe they have enough electronic know-how to have fixed up some kind of antibug warning device. From what I've found out so far, the Williams boy is pretty good in that field. It seems he had a friend who was even better—quite brilliant"—(Carlos was smiling proudly.)—"a kid who died last year—about the same time as David disappeared, as a matter of fact. . . ."

Danny whispered, "David? Who's David?"

Carlos and Karen shrugged. Joe frowned and shook his head.

"No, Larry. I'm quite certain there was no connection. The kid's death was some stupid mistake, working on a computer or something. Electrocuted himself." (Carlos scowled, muttering, "Stupid, huh?") "Anyway, it's only a matter of time before they find the bug. . . ." (Carlos nodded as if to say, "You can bet on that, too, buster!") "No. Before that happens, I propose to ask for their help. . . . Absolutely! Tomorrow. As soon after school as possible. . . . Oh, I'll find a way—don't worry!"

The ghosts looked at each other.

"We'll be there!" muttered Joe.

"Eh?" Gideon was smiling now. (And it was,

thought Karen, a very engaging smile.) "He did, huh? Well, I'm not surprised. He didn't look like the kind of man who'd be too easily satisfied. Typical lawyer. Anyway, I trust you told him I was one of your most promising young representatives?"

"That must be Mr. Williams he's talking about," said Karen.

Gideon started to laugh.

"Don't be too sure! I've already gotten three people definitely interested in the siding deal. Especially when I told them about the firm's special limited discount offer. . . ."

"We have to get word to Buzz and Wacko," said Karen.

"As soon as he's through," said Joe, not wanting to miss a single word, however innocent-seeming.

Gideon's face was serious again.

"No. You can get hold of me at the Lakeview Hotel. But remember—nothing sensitive. I don't trust *any* hotel switchboard, even back home. Just ask if I've heard from Aunt Gerda lately, and I'll slip out and get back to you over this pay phone. OK? OK, then. *Shalom.* . . ." Gideon's smile came back. "I'm glad to hear you know *that* word, at least! *Shalom aleichem!*"

"Well," said Karen as the man replaced the phone. "That tells us where he's staying. So there's no point in climbing back on *his* car."

"And I don't see any other," said Danny. "It looks like we'd better start walking if we're going to be in time for that after-dinner session at Wacko's."

The gas station clock registered 7:14. There seemed

no real chance that some other car, heading for town, would soon stop for gas. So, as ghosts can walk or run only at the speeds they were capable of when they were living normal lives, Danny's reminder was very timely.

"Let's move," said Joe. "We'll make it. We just *have* to, now!"

As they hurried back to town, they wondered exactly who the man Gideon was, and what kind of help he needed from Buzz and Wacko, and if he really could be trusted.

"And especially," Joe kept saying, "how on earth he knew it was Buzz who phoned in with that bomb plot warning to the Israeli consulate?"

8
Joe's Briefing

They needn't have worried about the time. Buzz himself happened to be about five minutes late, and they were able to accompany him in without any trouble when Wacko answered the door.

Up in Wacko's room, Carlos's first job was to relay a warning.

"Maintain full security precautions as before. Write or type all responses. Plus fill in with phony remarks about radio reception, or modifications to the FM circuit, or something like that."

When Wacko typed the reply, *"Why? Is he still snooping around?"*—Carlos told him they didn't think so, but they just couldn't afford to take unnecessary risks.

Then he went on to report all that had happened since leaving earlier.

At first, Buzz and Wacko tried to keep up the phony

conversation. But as the report unfolded, they fell silent, so that the only movement on their faces for minutes at a stretch was the reflected greenish flicker from the screen.

And when the report reached the man's phone call and his mention of Buzz's warning, the two boys were shocked into speech again.

"Hey, but how—?"

"Are you *sure* he—?"

"*Be quiet!*" The screen seemed to roar. "*Remember you might be overheard! Dummies!*"

They listened to the rest of the report without any further lapse. But by the end—especially when they learned that the man intended to question them face-to-face—they were seething with questions and comments. Then the word processor and Buzz's notepad worked overtime.

The first big question was how the man could possibly know that Buzz had made that call to the consulate back in July.

I mean, OK. Buzz wrote. *The guy is probably an Israeli himself. But you guys were given the tip-off about the bomb by a ghost, and how could she possibly have communicated with him? Could she have made some kind of breakthrough herself?*

They doubted it. They had met Irma Shavit at Heathrow Airport in London while working on the Jackman case. She had told them of the bomb plot—details of which she'd overheard—and she'd been terribly distressed. When they told her they *might* be able to help—pretending they could occasionally make

46

telepathic contact with the living—she had been grateful for the offer but not very hopeful.

"*No,*" came the reply to Buzz's question. "*She wasn't within a million light-years of being able to communicate the way we do. She must have flipped with joy when she realized we'd passed on the warning. Remember, her sister was on the plane that came so close to being blown up. But she had no way of telling anyone about it—anyone living.*"

"*Did you mention which town you came from?*" Wacko typed.

"*It wouldn't have made much difference if we had,*" Carlos replied. "*But all she knew was that we came from the U.S.*"

Buzz scribbled a question of his own.

And you didn't mention our names?

"*No way! Although we knew she couldn't communicate with any living person, there was still the danger that she might tell other ghosts. And we sure didn't want any of them snooping around. It might have attracted Malevs, wanting to muscle in on the act for their own purposes.*"

That produced a silence. Both boys knew that Malevs were the haters—the ghosts who stayed around in the hope of doing maximum harm to living enemies, plus anyone else they took a dislike to. Such ghosts found it very difficult to carry out vendettas against the living. But since ghosts can do just as much physical damage to other ghosts as living people can do to each other, the regular caring ghosts were very wary indeed about having anything to do with Malevs.

"*Anyway,*" came Carlos's next message, "*how about*

you, Buzz? Could you possibly have let your name slip out when you called the consulate?"

No way!! What do you take me for?

Then Wacko hit on the solution.

"Hey! Wait a second! Remember the day you made the calls, Buzz? One to Scotland Yard about Jackman and the other to the consulate about the bomb?"

Buzz nodded, looking at Wacko with a puzzled frown.

"Well, when you reported back, didn't you say something about the responses? How you were put through to the Scotland Yard people immediately, but the consulate kept you on hold?"

"Hey, yes!" Carlos said to the others. "*I* remember that now! 'They kept me on hold for a few minutes.' Those were his exact words!"

Buzz too had remembered.

Yes, he wrote. *So?*

"So that was it," Wacko typed. *"They must have put a trace on that call."*

"Could they do that?" Joe asked Carlos.

"Sure! If the call took long enough. And if they had the cooperation of someone at the phone company."

Joe nodded.

"OK. Tell Wacko he's probably right. But that that only answers one of our questions. Ask if *they* have any idea what might be going on at Camp Wednesday. Also if *they* know anything about a kid called David who disappeared some time in July of last year—possibly connected with Camp Wednesday."

"Is that it?" asked Carlos.

"No. The third and most important question is this. Are they willing to allow the stranger to interview them? I mean, we'll be there too. But remind them that we still don't know enough about the guy to trust him one hundred percent. I have a feeling he could be very dangerous if crossed."

The answers to the first two questions were thoughtful negatives.

Wacko himself still had unpleasant vibrations about the At-Home Day. But, other than that, he'd heard nothing especially bad about the camp.

As for the missing kid, well—not really. Somewhere at the back of Buzz's mind there was a vague memory. Some news item about *some* kid who'd run away from *some* camp in the area—but only as part of a more general plan to leave home for good, using the camp as a way station. Buzz ended by shaking his head as he scribbled his reply. He just couldn't remember any names or dates.

To the third question, however, the answer was a very rousing affirmative.

"You try and stop us!!!" Wacko typed.

Hear, hear! agreed Buzz, filling a whole page with *his* response.

"All right," said Joe, unable to restrain a slight tight smile of pride. "But tell them to take absolute maximum care. Suggest that they give the guy the opportunity he needs. Maybe by walking home from school instead of taking the bus. But *not* by accompanying him in his car. Or allowing him to draw them into any secluded place. Tell them to keep in the open, within view of other people and where it will be easy for us to stay close. And—"

"Sure thing! I'll—"

"Wait! And above all, warn them not to give too much away about themselves, and nothing—but *nothing*—about us. OK? Tell them to go along with his radio-interception theory, but to be very guarded about it. Like *that* was the secret they wanted to keep to themselves—some extraspecial radio equipment."

Carlos conveyed that message, the boys agreed to follow Joe's briefing right down the line and the ghosts departed—after wishing their living colleagues the very best of luck.

"Which they'll certainly need!" said Karen as they walked out into the driveway. She was thinking of the man called Gideon. "Whatever else he may be, that guy is no fool!"

None of the others disagreed. More than one pair of ghostly fingers was tightly crossed.

9
The Disappearance of David Rafferty

The following afternoon was very different from the previous one. There had been a sudden change in the weather overnight, and the sky was clear—golden in the west, lavender in the north and pink in the east. It was quite warm, too, giving an illusion of early spring.

To Buzz and Wacko, strolling home from school, it was difficult to believe there were such beings as ghosts and sinister prowling night visitors around. Even the town's main cemetery looked almost cheerful and parklike—stretching away to their right, with its lawns and glades and gravel walks, its splashes of color in flower vases and urns, and the sparkling white monuments rising above clumps of evergreens.

In fact, the only obvious sign of early winter was high overhead, where a long, long skein of faintly honking geese was heading south, with another, more distant line over to the west, suddenly veering, as if to converge with the nearer flock.

"There must be hundreds!" said Buzz, squinting up.

"Yeah," said Wacko. "They—"

Then he nearly collided with Buzz, after feeling a brief cool warning brush on his upper lip.

Almost immediately, a voice behind them said: "It's a wonder they don't interfere with radio reception, isn't it? All that mysterious energy that must go into *their* communications system."

"But—"

The boys had stopped and were staring at the man who had come up so quietly behind them. He was still staring up at the geese. He had shed his parka, but was wearing the same gray business suit and carrying the black briefcase.

He brought his eyes down. They were brown and clear and candid. His face gradually lit up with a broad smile.

"The geese," he said, glancing up. "I was talking about the geese."

"Oh—uh—yeah!" muttered Buzz.

He was wondering whether in fact this really was the guy they'd been warned about.

Gideon himself cleared that up.

"Hi!" he said. "I'm sorry if I startled you. *You'll* be Robert Phillips, yes? And *you* must be Henry Williams, right?"

They nodded. He still looked open and relaxed. It was hard to reconcile what they saw with the picture painted by the others.

"Good!" said the man. "I've been hoping to speak

with you. My name is Mishcon. I'm a private investigator, and I think you might be able to help me. I've
left my car a little way up the road and—"

Buzz had been the one to feel the warning touch
this time, but it hadn't been necessary.

"I'm sorry, Mr.—uh—"

"Mishcon. Gideon Mishcon."

"—Mr. Mishcon, but if you've anything to say to
us, I don't see why you shouldn't say it out here."

"After all," said Wacko, more tactfully, "it isn't often
we get a day like this, so late in the year. That's why
we decided to walk."

The man gave Wacko a look of respect.

"You're so right!" He glanced over the neat picket
fence, at the cemetery's lawns and paths. "Why don't
we take a turn in there? It looks very pleasant just now,
considering what it is."

There were a few people around, strolling along the
paths, bending to inspect the gravestones or arranging
fresh flowers in the vases.

Buzz and Wacko looked at each other. There'd been
no warning touch this time.

"Why not?" said Buzz.

They went in at the main entrance. Just inside, the
driveway split left and right, around a landscaped island with a large fountain as centerpiece. The water
jetted up from the middle of a wide copper bowl that
was constantly overflowing and spilling into a small
pond. It was a memorial to the dead of two world wars,
with benches on all sides, sheltered by clumps of dark
evergreen bushes.

"Shall we sit down here?"

There was only one other person there—an elderly woman at the other side of the fountain, feeding some noisy sparrows.

They sat down.

"How did you know our names?" said Wacko.

"It is my business to." The man wasn't smiling now, but he still looked relaxed. "You are in fact the key to my inquiry. In fact, I'm counting on your being able to help."

"Let's hope we can," said Buzz. "But—*what* inquiry?"

"Back in July," said the man, "you—Robert Phillips—made a phone call to the Israeli consulate in New York. Correct?"

Buzz blinked.

"I—uh—may have."

"You did. You were able to give a very valuable warning. About a bomb attack that was scheduled to take place in—or, more precisely, *over*—Tel Aviv." The man was staring straight ahead, as if reading matters of recorded fact from an invisible cue card. "I need not say how grateful the authorities were. You saved at least three hundred lives. So, of course, there's no need to be so—uh—wary—about admitting it."

"We've admitted nothing," said Wacko.

The man shot him a keen glance. He seemed to be surprised at the coolness of their response. Buzz wondered if it hadn't been *too* cool—betraying the fact that they'd been prepared for this.

The man turned and gazed across at the bird-feeding woman.

"If it's publicity you're worried about, forget it.

Government agencies never disclose their sources of valuable information. And, from what I've gathered, you fellows are particularly anxious to keep your—uh—methods—under wraps."

He was looking at them again, the smile slowly stealing back.

"Really?" said Wacko. "You seem to know a great deal, Mr. Mishcon. Why bother to ask us anything at all?"

The man's face turned serious.

"Because, Henry, something else has arisen. Something very important indeed. And we—my clients and I—think you can help."

"How?" said Wacko.

"Well, quite obviously you were able to intercept a message—probably a radio message—from or to a place not far from here. A message discussing the bomb plot."

"Not far from here?" Buzz couldn't resist a sly grin, which froze immediately with a touch on the lip. "Uh—you mean someplace in this locality?"

"I do," said the man. "Maybe you don't know *where*, exactly, but I can tell you we have every reason to believe it was Camp Wednesday."

"Oh?" Buzz pretended to be surprised. "You mean the summer camp out along Route 106?"

"Yes. The place to which the sixteen-year-old son of my clients, a boy called David Rafferty, went in late June last year. And from which he disappeared not many days later. I suppose you haven't intercepted any messages mentioning his name?"

The man gave them a careful look.

"No," said Wacko. "It was before"—there was a brief warning touch—"before we had the equipment, anyway."

"Long before," said Buzz.

"Did you read or hear anything about David Rafferty, at the time?"

They shook their heads.

The man opened the briefcase and took out a photograph.

"Does *this* ring any bells?"

It was a portrait of a kid of fifteen or sixteen. He had a long, thin pale face, with prominent cheekbones and a wide generous mouth. The lips were set in a rather fixed smile, and the brown eyes seemed to glow from under the light sandy eyebrows. His red hair looked wiry.

"David?" asked Buzz.

The man nodded.

"Recognize him at all? It appeared in several newspapers at the time."

They shook their heads again.

"Where did he come from?" asked Wacko. "And why do you suspect the people at Camp Wednesday?"

The man returned the picture (which had been keenly scrutinized by more than two pairs of eyes) to the briefcase.

"His home is—or was—in Kansas City. And, when he went to Camp Wednesday, I think he really did have the intention simply to use it as a jumping-off point for Boston or New York—hoping to sign on with a ship there, maybe. That was the theory at the time."

"Why would he do that?" said Wacko.

"Because he was crazy to go to Israel. It had been his one ambition for over a year. He wanted to join the army there. He'd tried—applying by mail and other means—several times, but he'd always been turned down. He was obviously too young, and his parents wouldn't hear of it. His father's Irish, by the way. It's his mother who's Jewish.

"Anyway, the first thing his parents did was to inform the police here about his ambition—and to have them watch the ports, the airports, anywhere he might have been heading en route to Israel. They even had the Israeli authorities checking at all *their* ports of entry. But—no David. No record of anyone even sighting him. So, that was that. Just another missing kid who'd probably fallen into the wrong sort of company on his way to fulfilling his ambition."

The man sighed.

"So why this new interest in Camp Wednesday?"

Gideon's smile was wry as he glanced at Buzz.

"Because of you, my friend."

"Me?"

"Yes. When investigations were set in motion to try and find out who had phoned in the bomb warning—from this area, remember—someone's memory was jogged. You see, there'd been another call to the consulate from here, almost exactly a year previously. So they hunted through the files and came up with the tape and compared it to some tapes David had made at home and—bingo!—it was the same kid. Voiceprints identical."

"What did he say?"

Gideon's eyes were hard now, as he gazed at the fountain.

"It was very short. And incomplete. Just twelve words. Ready for this?"

They nodded.

"The boy's voice, agitated, hardly more than a whisper, said, 'Listen, I think I've found the Ghoul of Grünberg. My name is—' "

Gideon made a clicking noise.

"And that was it. The line went dead. And—I'm very much afraid—so did David Rafferty, shortly afterward."

10
The Ghoul of Grünberg

Buzz cleared his throat. The stranger's disclosure had been more than he'd bargained for. But—could it really be true?

"The—the Ghoul of Grünberg?" he said. "Just who was—or is—he?"

Gideon sighed.

"You are very lucky that the name is *not* familiar to you. But—well—the Ghoul of Grünberg was the name given to the commandant of a Nazi SS death camp in what used to be eastern Germany, now part of Poland, during World War Two. His real name? Heinrich Mueller—the youngest man ever to—uh—rise to such a position. I won't go into details here—but he was directly responsible for the deaths of more than 150,000 people who passed through his camp."

"Yeah. I remember now," murmured Wacko. "Some

TV program. He escaped, right? Supposed to be hiding someplace in South America?"

"Escaped, yes. *South* America—doubtful."

"You mean—you think he might be *here*?" said Buzz. "In the *States*?"

"Yes."

"In this *area*? You mean David might *really* have stumbled into him?"

"Yes. In Camp Wednesday itself. In the person of Dr. Helmut Mendelssohn, no less." The wry smile reappeared."It's amazing, really. The way a person like that will go to such infinite pains to change his appearance, his manner, even his voice—but still cling to his initials. Criminals do it all the time. And I wouldn't be surprised if it turned out—quite unconsciously, of course—that he'd also clung to the initial letters of his beloved SS."

"Sir?"

"Science and Survival. The motto on the camp's sign."

"Well!"

The exclamation burst from Karen's lips.

She was standing right behind the man. The others were ranged alongside her, leaning forward.

"How about that?" murmured Joe.

"I think this guy's on the level!" said Carlos. "I think we should give him all the help we can!"

"Yeah," said Danny. "But that fat little guy last night—I don't see *him* killing all those people."

"Not even his men?" snapped Karen. "On his orders? I mean—"

60

"Be quiet!" growled Joe.

Wacko was speaking. He'd been trying to remember all he could about his short visit to Camp Wednesday.

"Do you know if David had any trouble enrolling there?"

"Not that I know of," said Gideon. "Why?"

"Being Jewish and all."

Gideon shook his head.

"Oh, I don't think Mueller would be stupid enough to show any discrimination *now*. Not *here*. Anyway, David took after his father in looks. Typically Irish. And with a name like Rafferty, no one would ever suspect him of being Jewish. In fact, if they *had*, it might have saved his life. They'd probably have been more careful about what they said when he was around."

Wacko nodded. He looked at Buzz inquiringly. Buzz nodded back.

"So what would you like us to do, Mr. Mishcon?"

"Whatever it was you did when you intercepted details of the bomb plot—which Mueller/Mendelssohn might very well have been privy to."

"But—" Wacko began.

"I'm not asking you to put yourselves in any danger, mind. I mean—well—let me ask you something." Gideon gave them a probing look. "What you found out about the bomb plot didn't involve your actually going *into* Camp Wednesday, did it?"

They gave him a very firm no.

"Good." Gideon looked genuinely relieved. "Because believe me—if Mendelssohn *is* Mueller, your lives wouldn't be worth a bent shekel if you were caught on a mission like that. . . . No. All I'm asking for is information. The slightest scrap, even, if it refers to David. All right?"

Wacko still had reservations.

"Why don't you—your clients—hand this over to the police or the FBI?"

The man shrugged.

"Both *were* involved when David disappeared. And they drew a blank."

"But didn't *they* know about David's aborted phone message?"

"Of course not. Even the Israelis didn't know who'd made the call. Not at the time. Besides, they probably weren't even aware of it. Not at a high enough level. Their consulates get thousands of calls every month from people who think they've sighted the Ghoul of Grünberg."

"Crackpots?"

"Some, yes. Plus well-meaning but mistaken persons. And especially around the time when some journalist happens to dig into the files and make a story of it. Around the time David called, for instance, there'd been yet another TV network special on the subject, and the consulate lines were jammed. All these calls get taped, of course, but they rarely get followed up unless something else happens to corroborate the suspicion."

"Like Buzz's call from the same area?"

"Exactly." Suddenly, the man laughed. "Hah! So you've admitted it directly, at last!"

"Well—"

"Anyway," said Gideon, serious again, with an almost pleading look, "how about it? Are you willing to help?"

"Before we answer that," said Wacko, "I have another question."

"Yes?"

"Now that you do have that extra corroboration, why don't you go back to the police or the FBI?"

The man gave him a slightly mocking smile.

"Well first, you realize that that would mean disclosing *your* part in reawakening those suspicions?"

"Oh, boy!" murmured Karen.

Wacko was shifting uneasily on the bench.

"Uh—I guess it would, at that."

"But don't worry," said Gideon. "Naturally, if I should uncover proof that Mendelssohn had something to do with David's disappearance, that would be the first thing I'd do. Take it to the authorities here. Then justice could take its course, and *everyone* would be satisfied. But in the meantime—before I have proof—no."

"Suppose we—you—didn't find any proof about David's disappearance?" said Wacko. "But you did find proof that Mendelssohn was the Ghoul of Grünberg?"

"Well, then we'd have to see," said Gideon, grimly.

"Would the Israelis kidnap him?"

"If they did, it would be to take him back for a fair trial. But that might not be possible. It isn't the present government's policy."

His eyes had become very hard. So hard that Buzz was moved to say, "There'd be no *illegal* action, would there? No executing him here, without a trial? Because—"

"There was no trial for those 150,000 people he exterminated," said Gideon, in a slow, grating voice. "They didn't even get a decent burial." He glanced around—at the woman feeding the birds, at the well-kept grounds, at the monuments turning gold in the setting sun—and he sighed. "But no. You needn't worry. Just concentrate on finding everything you can about David's disappearance. And if we find that Mueller had *him* exterminated, we will leave the rest to your own Justice Department, I promise you. OK? *Will* you help me?"

Again the boys looked at each other. They both wanted to say yes. But they waited for the touch that would confirm such a response.

It didn't come. The ghosts themselves were still not quite sure.

Buzz guessed that this was the case.

"Could we have some time to discuss—uh—to think it over?"

The man nodded.

"I suppose it *has* been dropped on you suddenly. . . . So—OK. This time tomorrow? Here?"

Then the boys felt touches—each on his right ear—the affirmative signal.

They nodded.

"Fine!" said Gideon, standing up. "Meanwhile, you promise not to breathe a word of my inquiry? To anybody?"

There was a slight hesitation. Then Buzz smiled.

"Not to a single living soul!"

"That was a neat reply!" said Karen as the man walked away and Buzz and Wacko watched him go.

"Well, you guys, *we'd* better be on our way too," said Wacko, getting up and looking at his watch. "How about five-thirty again?"

"We'll be there," said Joe—touching Wacko's right ear.

"Yes!" came a voice from behind a bush at the back of them. "And I hope you'll convince them that they'll be doing the right thing to give him all the help they can!"

At the first word, the four ghosts had spun around, horrified to think they'd been overheard—and obviously by another ghost.

Then Karen gave a little scream as the newcomer emerged.

"Irma!" she cried. "What are *you* doing here?"

11
Irma Comes Aboard

Sure enough, it was Irma Shavit. Even without her airline uniform, they would have recognized her by her glowing brown eyes, dark hair and the intense expression on her thin, fine-boned face. She was smiling now, otherwise she looked exactly the same as she had on their last meeting, in London. Then there had been no smile, only a look of great anxiety.

There was certainly nothing to show the effects of a long, five- or six-thousand-mile journey. Her hair was smooth, and there wasn't the slightest crease in her uniform. This was understandable, of course. Like all other ghosts, she was looking her best, and there wasn't even anything to indicate the mess she'd been in when they carried her off in a plastic bag, her body badly mangled by terrorists' bullets and hand grenades.

Even so, Karen couldn't help being impressed.

"You're looking great, Irma!" she said.

"Yeah," murmured Joe. He glanced over his shoulder, glad to see that Buzz and Wacko were already turning into the street, but wondering nevertheless how much Irma had heard. "But, say, Irma—this *is* a surprise. What brings you here?"

Irma's smile broadened.

"Come, Joe—can't you guess?"

"Uh—you wanted to thank us for passing on the bomb warning?" said Joe, hopefully.

"Well, yes. That too. Of course!" Irma's eyes shone as she glanced around at them. "Thank you, all of you! From the bottom of my heart!"

But then her smile faded.

"Mainly, however, I have come about this matter of the Ghoul beast—and David Rafferty. I—I thought I might be able to assist."

"Ah—well—sure!" said Joe, his head seething with all the new problems her appearance had created. "But we do have the business well in hand."

"Do you? Really?"

A half-hearted murmur went around the others.

"Well—" Even Carlos couldn't find any enthusiastic words in reply. He shrugged and gazed at his feet.

"It's all right, Carlos," said Irma, smiling again. "There are very few people who could feel they were on top of a case like this. Not even Gideon."

They looked up.

"You know him, then?" said Joe.

"But of course! He is why I am here—why I knew where you lived."

"Oh?" said Karen. "Don't tell us you've found out how—how to—"

"Communicate with him?" Irma shook her head. "No, alas! Not even with the sort of code you seem to be using." (Joe gave a faint sigh of relief.) "But I overheard him discussing the mission. Back home, in Israel. And I realized at once that *you* were involved. And exactly where you were."

"Mission?" said Danny. "You mean the case he's working on? The missing kid?"

"As a private investigator? No, Danny. That is just a blind. Like his insulation-salesman cover. Gideon is really an agent in the *Shin Beth*."

"What's that?" said Carlos.

"The special branch—Israeli General Security Service. Though Gideon works for a *very* special section within that branch. He is a very capable agent—one of the best. But"—she shook her head—"in a case like this, I figured he needed every bit of help he could get."

Joe felt relieved. He'd already begun to feel a strong liking for Gideon. Only the man's evasiveness had made Joe so cautious.

"Sure," he said. "I guess you're right, Irma."

But he still wasn't happy about Irma's coming so close to the secret. She meant well, obviously. And she would never do anything to harm them. But there was always the risk of an accidental disclosure.

He decided to stall.

"How did you get here?" he asked.

"Oh—planes, planes, more planes—buses, private

cars, farm pickup trucks. It isn't hard to steal rides when you're a ghost. But"—she sighed—"this is one very large country you have here."

Karen frowned.

"But why all those vehicles, Irma? We're less than a hundred miles from Kennedy Airport. Don't tell me *you* lost your way!"

Irma laughed.

"Of course not! What kind of a flight attendant do you take me for? No. . . . I decided to go to Kansas City first."

"Kansas City?" said Joe.

"Yes. Where David Rafferty's mother and father live. Didn't you know that?"

Quickly, Joe calculated that unless Irma was lying, she couldn't have been behind the bush all of the time.

"Yes, but why go there?"

"I see you *can* use some help, Joe!" said Irma. Then she became serious. "Just think for a moment. David's parents were very distressed at his disappearance—his mother especially."

"So?"

"So wouldn't it be likely that if he *is* dead, his ghost would probably be there, in Kansas City, trying to comfort his mother?"

"Wow! Yeah!" murmured Danny.

"Good thinking," said Joe. "And—was he?"

"No. I guess after eighteen months—"

Irma broke off. Joe had just hit the palm of his left hand with his right fist.

"Sorry!" he said. "But—hey!—listen! If David was

so fanatical in his ambition to help the Israelis, maybe he chose to stay around Camp Wednesday!"

"Gosh, yes!" said Karen. "Hoping to nail the Ghoul of Grünberg! Giving that the top priority!"

"Which is exactly what I decided," said Irma. "Have you seen anything of him?"

They shook their heads.

"But of course we haven't been looking," said Joe. "We didn't even know about David until the last hour or so."

Irma flashed them a smile.

"So maybe I *can* help! Yes?"

Joe had been thinking very hard. Irma's help could be invaluable. She'd proved that already. And she would be especially useful in monitoring Gideon's activities, a man whose background she already knew so well. And *that* would keep her busy at those crucial times when they had to consult Buzz and Wacko.

Why not?

"Irma," he said, putting out his hand. "You're on. Welcome aboard!"

70

12
The Double Whammy

After they'd all shaken hands, Joe got down to business.

"Do you know where Gideon is staying?"

"Sure," said Irma. "They decided back in Jerusalem that the Lakeview Hotel would be the best place. In fact, that is where I went when I arrived this morning. It took some finding, and I was hoping I might run into one of you. But I managed."

Joe's eyes narrowed.

"Did you follow Gideon *here*?"

"Yes. But I was—well—somewhat delayed."

Joe felt relieved. Maybe she hadn't seen or heard too much, after all.

"What has he been doing all day?" Karen asked.

"Well, mainly going about his cover business," said Irma. "Insulation and siding."

"Is he *that* conscientious?" asked Joe.

"Believe it! Gideon is one of the most meticulous operatives in *Shin Beth*. He likes to live the parts he has to play. And today it was especially important."

"Why?" said Danny.

Irma shrugged.

"Oh, it seems some private citizen had been suspicious about his activities lately. Reporting Gideon to the police. A Mr. Williams."

"*What?*"

Joe's eyes had popped. The others were gaping, too.

"How do *you* know that?" asked Karen.

"I was there, at the hotel," said Irma. "When the policeman came. A plainclothes detective."

"Oh, no!" Danny groaned. "It wouldn't be—"

"A Detective Grogan," Irma was saying. "That's how he announced himself. Do you know him?"

Did they know Detective Grogan!

This was a double whammy, indeed.

"You bet we do!" said Danny. Catching a warning look from Joe, he went on, more slowly: "He—he once suspected me of having something to do with a break-in at school. Before I was killed." Joe gave him an approving nod. Danny continued with more confidence. "Just because I predicted the break-in. Grogan thought I must have had inside information. My friend, Buzz Phillips, too."

"Phillips? *Robert* Phillips? The boy who telephoned the warning? The one who was here just now?"

Irma looked very interested. *Too* interested, Joe thought. He hoped Danny wouldn't be foolish enough to tell her how Buzz and Wacko had continued to arouse Grogan's suspicions, even after Danny's death.

How, every time the Ghost Squad had unearthed something that had to be reported to the police, Grogan suspected them of holding something back—especially the source of their information.

Danny was surging on.

"Sure. You see, I used to have this knack—this gift—of being able to dream about the future. Not every night. And not *exactly* what was going to happen. It was all sort of—uh—wrapped up, disguised."

"And Buzz—Robert—" said Irma. "Where did he come in?"

"Oh, he was the interpreter! He used to figure the dreams out. I wasn't any good at that, myself."

"I see," murmured the newcomer. "So there always *was* a kind of telepathic link between you and him."

"Yeah, well—" Danny grinned bashfully. (Joe had just given him a slow wink, half-approving, half-warning.) "I suppose you could call it that, Irma, yeah. But," he added, suddenly modest, "Carlos has an even stronger link with Wacko."

Joe winced, but Irma nodded.

"So *that's* the reason you've been able to make such good progress with your communications system!" Then, noticing their embarrassed looks, she smiled. "Don't worry. Your secret is safe with me."

"It doesn't always work," said Carlos, catching on. "Very often it—"

"Anyway," said Joe, cutting in while they were ahead of the game, "how did Gideon make out with Detective Grogan?"

"Oh, quite well! His credentials were perfectly in

order. The head of the Polinsulation firm is a very great friend to our country, and he's provided a complete backup for Gideon. The detective seemed quite satisfied. He even made jokes about nervous citizens reporting innocent activities as suspicious behavior. But these days, he said, it was better to be safe than sorry." Irma smiled. "And Gideon agreed. Wholeheartedly. 'One can't ever be too careful, officer!' he said. And he meant it, too."

"Yeah," Joe murmured, recollecting the way Gideon had handled himself the previous night.

"So I wasn't surprised when he went out and threw himself into his cover job," said Irma. "He's been trying to sell insulation all day. He didn't even break for lunch. Then he went straight to the school and watched for the boys, ready to follow the bus in his car, if necessary. I suppose he—how do you say it?—lucked out—when they decided to walk."

"So you were with him when he followed them here?" said Joe.

"Most of the way, yes. Until I thought I caught sight of Detective Grogan, in a car, following *him*. That's why I was delayed. I wanted to make sure."

"And *was* Grogan following *him*?" said Joe, alarmed.

"No. I was mistaken."

"Let's hope so!" sighed Joe. "Anyway," he said, more briskly, "you think we should help Gideon?"

"Oh, most certainly!" said Irma. "That Ghoul of Grünberg was a horrible man. And he could still be mixed up in anti-Jewish activities, even now. He *must* be stopped. He is so terribly clever, especially with electronics."

"You mean using the stuff at Camp Wednesday?"

"Yes," said Irma. "But I am also thinking of his record at the camp in Grünberg. Did you know he experimented with the effects of electricity on humans? Shock treatment, torture, the chemical reaction of human tissue to various currents. Horrible!"

Karen shuddered.

"Irma's right! We just *have* to help!"

Joe nodded.

"There's no question of our not helping. So let's get right on it, huh?" He'd been thinking about keeping their secret safe, as well as bringing the Ghoul to book. Now he thought he could see his way to dealing with both problems so that they wouldn't clash. "Listen, Irma," he said. "Gideon has probably gone back to the hotel already. Do you know how to get back there on foot from here?"

Irma looked rather uneasy.

"Well, I can do what I did this morning, I suppose. . . ."

Joe shook his head.

"Not good enough." He turned. "Karen, why don't you go with Irma? Show her the most direct route?"

"Well, sure," said Karen, smiling, but looking rather doubtful. "But—"

"Then maybe if Gideon is resting up," said Joe, "and there's nothing useful you could be doing there, maybe you could take Irma on—to Camp Wednesday itself—"

"Oh, but I'd love that!" said Irma.

"—and see if you can see anything of David Rafferty," Joe went on. "We'll join you there later, after we've tried to make some kind of contact with Buzz and Wacko."

Karen got the message.

"Sure!" she said. "I only hope you'll do better than last time."

Then they went their separate ways—Karen and Irma to the Lakeview Hotel, the others to Wacko's house.

Carlos, for one, felt glad to be leaving the cemetery. It was getting dark in there now. The bird lady had long since left, the sparrows had gone to roost, and now that the place had been deserted by the living, the shadows were beginning to get to him.

After all, that was the cemetery where he and some of the others were buried—what was left of their physical remains, anyway—and it was a thought that Carlos didn't care to dwell upon!

13
Wolfgang
Takes It Easy

The temperature dropped quickly in the early evening, and mist began to form in hollows and along the courses of rivers and streams. By 8:30, the mist was especially thick down by the lake at Camp Wednesday, completely enshrouding the statue.

"They don't seem to be down here anywhere," said Joe.

"Shall we give them a shout?" asked Carlos.

"No! We don't want to alert anyone else too soon." Danny grinned.

"Aren't you forgetting something, Joe? Living persons can't hear us, no matter how loud we yell."

"I wasn't thinking about living persons," said Joe as they began to move cautiously up the hill, out of the mist, to where the campers' cabins loomed dark against the stars.

"But why don't you want to alert Karen and Irma?"

said Danny. "We might waste hours just creeping around, waiting to catch sight of them."

"If they're here at all!" said Carlos. "They might have gotten shut in at the hotel."

He was feeling a little miffed. He had dearly wished to find Gideon's bug, somewhere in or around Wacko's room, but Joe had told him to forget it and concentrate on operating the word processor.

"We can use the same method as last time," he had said.

So Carlos had been kept busy, making sure that Buzz and Wacko were fully informed about the latest developments, and coping with their torrent of questions when they learned that Irma had turned up and that Detective Grogan might still be sniffing around on the track of Gideon.

"Make sure you warn Gideon, when you see him tomorrow afternoon," had been the final instructions. *"Tell him that Grogan is a whole lot smarter than he might seem."*

Now, as they made their way around the corner of the administration building, Joe said: "I wasn't thinking about Karen and Irma, either. I was thinking about not alerting David Rafferty."

"Oh, yeah, him!" Carlos nodded. "I guess if he's been haunting Camp Wednesday all on his own for eighteen months, he *could* be kind of shy about strange ghosts suddenly showing up."

"Exactly!" said Joe, dryly.

"So what if Karen and Irma have already scared him?" said Danny.

"Or maybe even found him?" said Carlos.

78

"We should be so lucky!" muttered Joe. "Come on, let's take a look up at the Director's Residence."

As on their previous visit, there were a few lights glimmering through the trees on the hill. Even Danny began to feel more hopeful as they walked up the private driveway.

"I bet the director's house is where David's ghost will spend the most time," he said. "Trying to get back at his murderers."

"Yeah," grunted Joe. "If he *was* murdered here. We still don't have any hard evidence of that."

"I wonder what methods he's been trying," said Carlos. "If he *was* murdered here."

"Something pretty futile," said Joe. "Without our help—and Buzz and Wacko's—I can't see any ghost standing much chance. Unless he's an out-and-out Malev by now. Raring for revenge can make even a decent guy—ghost or living—turn very nasty."

They were getting close to the house. There was enough light from various windows to reveal that it was a large three-story Victorian building, with all kinds of fancy turrets and gables.

Danny gulped. The thought that the ghost they had come to help might turn out to be a vicious Malev made him inspect the shadows more intently.

"What if—?" he began.

Then he nearly died a second death.

"*Boo!*" growled a figure, jumping out from behind a bush.

"Karen!" said Joe, his fist arrested in midswing. "You play ghosts with ghosts, and you're liable to get hurt!"

"S-sorry!" said Karen, fighting back her desire to giggle. "I—I just couldn't resist. And—oh boy!—the look on D-Danny's face! A-a-and *yours!*"

She ended on a squeal of laughter.

"I tried to stop her," said Irma, coming out from behind the same bush. "But—but—oh dear!—you did look funny—all of you!"

Then she too burst into laughter.

The girls had obviously been getting on well together—and both were relieved to discover that they *could* hit it off. That, decided Joe, was the reason for this giddiness. But it was something he could have done without, and his reaction was deliberately sour.

"OK! Calm down, you two!" Then, crisply: "How've you been making out? Have you learned anything new?"

His quick change of tone had its effect. Soberly, they shook their heads.

"We haven't been here long enough," said Irma. "Only about ten minutes."

"How about you guys?" said Karen. "Did you manage to get anything through to Buzz and Wacko?"

"Some," said Joe. "We managed to convey to them that it's OK to give Gideon all the help they can."

"And they understood?" said Irma.

"We think so. Hope so, anyway. . . . I assume you've not seen anything of David?"

They shook their heads.

"Any other ghosts who might be likely to give us some useful information?" said Joe.

"Ah, well—" said Karen, brightening up. "We might

have. A woman. In the yard of a house farther along Route 106, on the boundary of this property. I'm surprised you didn't notice her yourselves."

They shook their heads.

"She may have gone around to the back of the house by the time you came by," Irma suggested, tactfully.

"Must have," grunted Joe. "Anyway, who was she?"

Karen frowned.

"I'm afraid she doesn't look like she'll be much of a help, really. She's one of your typical *place* haunters."

"Oh, boy!" groaned Carlos.

The others looked equally disappointed.

They all knew what Karen meant by *that*. . . .

Contrary to popular opinion, ghosts usually haunt persons, not places. Before forming the Ghost Squad, the missions of the four nonliving members had been exclusively centered on the survivors: People they had cared for a lot. People who were missing them so much that they were making themselves sick. Or people who had depended on them a great deal and were likely to flounder without them.

Danny, for instance, had stayed around to try to give comfort to his four younger brothers and sisters. Karen's mission had been to try to convey the message to her father—a nervous wreck—that it had not been his fault that she had been run over by the truck, while running an errand for him. Joe himself had been deeply concerned to convince his wife that he had *not* committed suicide in that construction-site fall. As for Carlos, his passion for his electronics experiments had

81

been so great that he hadn't been able to bear the thought of leaving them unfinished—knowing that Wacko would never have been able to cope with them on his own.

At the core of all these assorted missions, even Carlos's, there had been one common element: persons. But place haunters are only negatively concerned with people. To them, the place is everything, whether it be a beautiful old garden, or house, or monastery, or church. Even a ruin. Even a desolate stretch of countryside. The only time *they* start taking an interest in people is when people threaten their beloved place— either with plans for tearing it down, or building on it, or harming it in some other way. Then, in their attitude to such intruders, the place haunters can soon find themselves behaving like Malevs.

Joe was very keen to learn what type this woman might be.

"Is she just the placid kind, do you think? Simply content to hang around and think about the time she lived there?"

"No way!" said Karen. "She had a real beef against the present owners. *And* about the Camp Wednesday people."

"Really?" said Joe. "What kind of beef?"

"Oh, something to do with her old house," said Karen, shrugging. "She says the new owners are thinking of selling the property to Mendelssohn, and she hates the idea."

"Why?" said Carlos. "Does she know something about him? Something bad? Something we might be able—?"

"No, no!" Irma was shaking her head. "Unfortunately . . . She thinks her old place might be turned into a squash court or something that will require drastic alterations. And she is so focused on the new owners—trying to *will* them to change their minds, poor woman!—that she rarely notices anyone or anything else."

"Not unless they go right up to her," said Karen. "Like we did, tonight."

"That is what she *said*, anyway," Irma added. "When we asked if she'd seen anything of David."

"You think she might have been lying?" said Danny.

"No," said Irma. "She was far too obsessed with her problem to try to cover up for anyone else. But maybe something will occur to her, if we keep trying. Ghosts have such terribly selective memories. Everything happening around us, after death, soon becomes blurred in our memories, unless connected directly to our missions."

They nodded. Their decision to form the Ghost Squad had done much to widen their focus. The mission to fight crime generally had made them much more alert to matters unrelated to their narrower individual concerns.

"But," said Irma, "don't look so glum. The fact that her memory for other things is blurred doesn't mean it is nonexistent. We must be patient. Visit her again. Try to coax those memories out of the mist."

"Yeah," murmured Danny, "and hope they *are* useful."

"It's worth a try, anyway," said Joe. "Thanks, you two. You did well." He turned and looked at the house.

"Meanwhile, let's see if we can pick up something useful from the suspects themselves."

"Not much hope of that," said Karen as they approached the nearest lighted window. "It's Dullsville in there, right now. Just a quiet evening home by the fireside."

"Hm!" Joe murmured. "I see what you mean."

The drapes had been left open, and the watchers all had an excellent view of the room. It was long, with a high ceiling, and its width was in proportion. But it had so many pictures, mirrors, banners and the heads of stuffed animals ranged along the walls that at first sight the room looked much smaller than it really was. A huge fire blazed in its recess on the wall opposite the window, and, on a couch that was placed slantwise in front of it, reading a book and absentmindedly scratching the ears of the Doberman, a man was reclining.

Despite the fact that they had a clear view of one side of his head, it took a few seconds for some of them to recognize him.

"Oh—uh—yeah . . ." Joe said. "That *is* Wolfgang—isn't it?"

"Yes," said Karen.

"Wolfgang Schrader," said Irma.

"You've seen him before?" asked Carlos.

Irma shook her head.

"No. But the name is familiar. It was mentioned at Gideon's briefing. It is believed that he was Mueller's personal body servant, his batman, at the camp in Grünberg. Staff sergeant Wilhelm Schmidt."

"I bet *he* hasn't changed all that much!" said Joe, watching the muscular forearm and the long powerful, slowly scratching fingers.

Irma shrugged.

"There's no way of knowing. It seems there are no photographic records of him on file." She smiled. "But the new name was enough to convince Gideon. He has a theory about initials—"

"We heard it," said Joe. "I must say old Wolfgang or Wilhelm or whatever is taking it darned easy. Maybe Mendelssohn's having a night off. Did you see anything of him, either of you?"

The girls shook their heads. Then:

"He wouldn't like *that!*" said Karen as Wolfgang raised his left leg higher and placed the foot—still in its large lace-up workman's boot—on a silk cushion.

"What was the name of the camp at Grünberg?" asked Carlos, marveling at the docile look of both dog and man. The dog was squeezing its eyes as it laid its chin on the man's thigh. The man's half-moon reading glasses made him look more like somebody's still active but gentle old granddad, leafing through an L. L. Bean catalogue. "Did *that* have the same initials?"

"As Camp Wednesday?" said Irma. Her face became stern. "No. Some typically Nazi bureaucratic cover-up name. Like Rehabilitation Center for Racial Delinquents." Then, with an effort, she let her face relax. "But the name Camp Wednesday was considered interesting anyway."

"How?" said Joe.

"Well, according to the official camp booklet, Wednesday was the day on which the good, grateful Dr. Mendelssohn, refugee from East German tyranny, first set foot on American soil. Back in 1953."

"So?"

"Well, Gideon thinks the choice of name had more to do with Wotan, the old German god who gave his name to the day."

"Why should that have significance for a guy like Mendelssohn—or Mueller?"

"Because Wotan was the god of wisdom, culture, *war*"—here Irma's voice became harsher—"and the *dead.*"

The others fell silent. It was a creepy thought.

Karen cleared her throat.

"Well—uh—it's peaceful enough in there just now, anyway."

"Yeah," grunted Joe. "It's obviously in the wisdom and culture phase."

Carlos laughed.

"It wouldn't be peaceful if he knew he was being watched by the *dead!* Anyway, come on. We can't stop here all night watching a guy read a book. Let's see what's going on at the other windows."

But there they were unlucky. The drapes were closely drawn at the only other first-floor lighted window around the side. And although there was a dimmer light on the second floor, at the back, and it was undraped, it seemed to be no more than a landing window.

"What about this one?" said Danny as they moved

around to the front again. He was pointing to a crack of light that seemed to be coming from the ground. "Looks like a basement window. Heavily barred, too."

But, try as they might, none of them could see far enough into the room there, through the chink at the side of the heavy drapes.

"Seems like an old black-and-white television's on," said Carlos, noticing a bluish white flickering. "Or— hey, yeah!—maybe a *bank* of TV screens!"

"Security-monitoring system?" said Joe.

"It wouldn't surprise me," said Carlos, remembering the previous evening and Wolfgang's sudden appearance.

"Anyway, *we* won't be showing up on it!" said Karen.

Carlos gave up on the crack, and they went on their way, back to the first window.

Wolfgang was still reading.

"Maybe Mendelssohn is in one of those other rooms," said Irma. "I do wish he'd come into this one. I'd—"

As if in answer to her wish, the camp director had just walked in. He was wearing a smart black velvet jacket, and his plump face had the same calm, slightly amused look they'd seen before.

What surprised them, though, was the fact that this expression remained the same.

For, not only did Wolfgang ignore him, he made no attempt to get up. He even continued to read the book when Mendelssohn said something to him—some words none of them could catch. A slight shake of the shoulders told them that Wolfgang had responded with a grunt.

Then Mendelssohn crossed to a corner cabinet. Opening it, he took out a small silver tray, a bottle of colorless liquid and a single glass. He brought these toward the man on the couch and said something else.

Without looking up, Wolfgang negligently waved in the direction of a nearby coffee table. Mendelssohn nodded, his face less genial—in fact with a rather spiteful side-glance at the reclining man. Then he set the tray on the table and moved it within Wolfgang's reach.

Having done that, he left the room.

In all this time, only the dog had deigned to look at him, and that was with pricked ears and a mildly suspicious gaze.

"Now *that*," murmured Joe, "was very interesting!"

"Yes," said Irma. "Given their relationship, I should say it was downright insolence!"

"Yet Mendelssohn didn't seem to mind all that much," said Carlos. "It looks like Heinrich Mueller *has* changed a lot!"

"Maybe," said Joe. "Maybe not. I mean, how would it be if he knew he just *had* to put up with that behavior? Either that, or be denounced as a much-wanted war criminal?"

"Blackmail?" said Karen.

"It sure seems like it," said Joe.

Irma's eyes were glowing.

"It is something Gideon will be very interested to hear about," she said. "It could be the lever that will help to crack open the whole case!"

They made one other visit on their way back to town, later. They stopped by at the house on 106. Its terraced gardens and immaculate lawns looked lovely in the moonlight.

But the one who loved these things the most was no longer there, outside, slowly circling around, sighing, stooping to inspect her former treasures. Since Karen and Irma had spoken with her, she had managed to get inside the house.

There was a lighted first-floor window here, too—and when they looked through, they saw another seemingly peaceful domestic scene.

A middle-aged couple were sitting on a love seat, laughing at some TV comedy show.

The ghosts, however, couldn't see what show it was.

That was because another ghost was standing directly in front of the screen, her arms folded, scowling at the two living viewers. They, of course, were completely unaware of her presence, since ghosts can only block the view of other ghosts.

Carlos grinned at the fat, elderly, scowling place haunter.

"You'll never get anywhere *that* way, lady!" he said, softly.

"And even if she did get through and scare them," said Karen, "she'd find it self-defeating. They'd be so terrified, they'd only hurry along their plans to sell the place—even if they lost money on the deal."

"We'll bear her problem in mind, though," Joe said. "If we can convince her that we may be able to help her solve it, she might get relaxed enough to remember what's been going on around her."

Judging from the woman's scowl and blazing eyes, it seemed to the others to be a very long shot as they went on their way. But—as events were to prove—it turned out to be very well worth taking.

So well worth taking, in fact, that had they realized it then, they would have sat around there until morning or even longer, waiting for the angry and frustrated place haunter to emerge.

14
Joe and Carlos Get Shut In

Next morning, the four ghosts split up.

Karen and Irma were detailed to follow Gideon. Danny was sent to the police headquarters to keep track of Grogan, just in case. And Joe and Carlos went early to Wacko's house, hoping to deliver an advance bulletin about what they'd discovered.

"It would help to let Gideon know as soon as possible about the blackmail angle," Irma had said.

"We'll see what we can do before Wacko leaves for school," said Joe. "Otherwise, it'll have to be late afternoon, after the meeting."

"Why?" Irma looked at him curiously. "Can't you get the message across while they're in school? It *is* rather important."

Carlos frowned and said, "Yeah, well—it's kind of difficult there. Too many kids around. Too much— uh—psychic interference."

"But we'll try," said Joe.

What they needed, of course, was to catch Wacko in his room and use the word processor. And at first it seemed they might succeed. Mr. Williams left for work early, and they were able to slip into the house at 7:30, when Mr. Williams paused at the open front door, on his way out.

But after that, their luck ran out.

The door to Wacko's room was shut. They heard him yawning. Then Carlos made the fatal mistake of suggesting they'd wait for him in the nearby bathroom and give him the alert sign there.

"He'll be heading straight for here anyway," said Carlos. "And we might not have time to slip into his room if he comes out in a hurry. Plus he's never wide enough awake before he showers. He might not even feel the warning before that."

It sounded reasonable. The door of the bathroom was open. It was the only bathroom on that floor. Wacko didn't have to share it with anyone.

So they went in and waited, and listened when Mrs. Williams came up and hammered on Wacko's door, telling him he was running late. Then, to their horror, she stopped outside the bathroom, shut the door and said: "And remember—you're not to use this bathroom until the plumber's been here!"

"OK, Mom," came Wacko's sleepy voice. "But how many more days is he gonna be, for Pete's sake?"

"He should be coming later this morning," said Mrs. Williams, already on her way downstairs.

The next half hour was agonizing.

They heard Wacko padding past the door, without being able to do anything about it. They heard him return from the second-floor bathroom, fully awake and humming a tune. They heard him pass again, on his way down to breakfast. They heard him say, "So long, Mom! See you this afternoon!" Then the quietness, with just a few distant kitchen sounds to emphasize it.

And that first busy spell was nothing compared to the ordeal that faced them now that they realized they were trapped, without even the chance that someone might rush in to grab a spare tube of toothpaste or something.

"Oh, boy!" sighed Carlos. "Let's hope the plumber arrives early!"

Joe groaned.

"Plumbers *never* arrive early! But"—he shrugged—"there's no point in fretting. Let's go over the case so far, see what we've managed to dig up."

They did this. Again and again.

By late morning, Carlos grew very restless.

"Isn't there something we can dislodge?" he said, looking around at the glass shelves. "Something that'll make a big enough crash to have Mrs. Williams running up to see what's happened?"

Joe sighed. Sometimes a ghost will find something just poised, teetering, at the edge of a shelf or table—something needing only the slightest brush to send it over. Then, if the ghost is expert at applying his micro-micro-energy to physical things, that final touch can be his.

Joe was such an expert. But experts are the first to recognize the impossible.

"No," he said. "I guess Wacko is just too tidy to leave anything in that state."

By early afternoon, Carlos was getting desperate.

"It looks like that plumber isn't coming at *all!* We'll miss the meeting. Even when Wacko and Buzz come back, they might never open *this* door!"

Joe frowned. He'd been staring at the bottom of the door, where there was a slight gap.

"There's *one* way, of course."

Carlos turned from the bathroom cabinet which he'd been inspecting.

"Huh?" Then he saw the direction of Joe's gaze. "Oh, no! Not that! Don't tell me you're thinking of doing a—*a Mickey Mouse?*"

Carlos had hesitated even to use the expression. His face was distorted with a mixture of horror and something else—a sort of shrinking disgust.

Joe winced and shook his head.

"No. Forget it. It would have to be a very great emergency for that. Nothing less than a matter of life and death."

Neither spoke for fully fifteen minutes. In the ghost world, what had come to be known as doing a Mickey Mouse, or Mickey Mousing, was so horrible—for both perpetrator and beholder—that it hardly bore thinking about.

"I tried it once, just with my hand, as an experiment," said Carlos, eventually, in a low faltering voice. "But—"

"That's enough!" snapped Joe, looking sick. "Quit it!"

Carlos nodded, gulped and fell silent.

It wasn't until around 2:45 that they were released from the bathroom, when the plumber finally arrived and was shown in by Mrs. Williams—saying he'd had to go all the way to Waterbury to get the special sealing compound.

And it wasn't until 3:15 that they were able to slip out of the house itself, when the plumber had to go to his truck and collect some tool he'd forgotten.

"Yippee!" cried Carlos, skipping down the driveway. "I told ya not to worry, Joe! You win some, and you lose some!"

"That's plumbers!" sighed Joe—grinning nevertheless.

Karen and Irma had spent a much less frustrating time.

First, they had a pleasant morning ride on Gideon's car, touring the Camp Wednesday area. They didn't go inside the camp's grounds, but slowly circled its borders, stopping off at a gas station, a drugstore in a small township near the camp's northern edge, and a coffee-shop bus stop to the south.

Gideon didn't enter any of these places to make purchases. All he did was go to the outdoor pay phones there and make the same call from each.

"I am now using the telephone at—" Here he gave the location and number. After that, he said nothing for two minutes. Nor, apparently, did he hear anything in reply, for he held the receiver well away from his face.

Then he would sign off by saying, "I will make the same call from this booth between 23:30 hours and 00:30 tonight."

"What was all *that* about?" said Karen, after the third call.

"I think I know," said Irma. "The number was a special line to the Israeli consulate. He is probably having them tape the background noise. They must be trying to identify the exact location from which David made his last call. It was made just after midnight, but I guess they are being thorough and checking at different times."

"I'll say they're thorough!" Karen glanced at Gideon with renewed admiration.

Irma nodded.

"Believe it!" she said. Then: "My guess is that David was using this one—hoping to catch a late bus—when they caught him."

"It would figure, I suppose," said Karen. "But why didn't the consulate people trace *David's* call?"

"Too short," said Irma. "Like the poor kid himself, they didn't have a chance!"

They spent the next few hours at the public library, where Gideon settled down to some further important research.

First, he examined a file of local weekly newspapers for the months of June, July and August of the previous year. He went through them line by line, column by column, page by page, including even the small ads. Making notes, he dwelt especially on:

1. An item concerning David's disappearance, with a fuzzy reproduction of the photograph Karen had already seen.

2. A short follow-up item saying it was believed that David had headed for Boston or New York "in pursuit of a preexisting ambition" and that (here Irma's lip curled) "it certainly had nothing to do with his few days at Camp Wednesday, which cabin-mates there say he seemed to be thoroughly enjoying."

3. A larger item, about the unveiling of the statue on the island, showing a beaming Dr. Mendelssohn shaking hands with the dignitary who'd come to perform the ceremony. This was an alumnus of the camp, now a three-star general with the Pentagon, "specializing in advanced communications systems." Gideon made a very special note of *his* name.

4. A two-page spread about the At-Home Day, with various pictures of the campers at work and at play. Counselors and staff appeared in some of them, and Dr. Mendelssohn in most. Wolfgang, however, was nowhere to be seen. The chief interest here was expressed by Karen and Irma—over a picture showing visitors watching some campers operating computers.

"Isn't that—?" Irma began.

"Yes!" said Karen, smiling. "Wacko and Carlos. Doesn't Carlos look wistful!"

"Wistful?"

"Well, by the time that was taken, he'd probably

realized that a summer at Camp Wednesday wasn't for *them!*"

It wasn't a good picture of Wacko, who had had his head half-turned from the camera, and Gideon seemed unaware that this was one of the boys he was due to meet later that day. Carlos's features were of course totally unknown to him, Karen decided.

5. The weekly roundup of police incident reports. Gideon paid particular attention to one of these—about a damaged phone booth, where the receiver had been dragged off the wall but not stolen. But then he shook his head when he realized it was located at the other end of the county.

"It wasn't the right date, either," said Irma.

Gideon's second line of research was less locally orientated.

After returning the newspaper files, he went into the lending department and browsed around the shelves. Eventually, having come across a picture in a book that seemed to interest him greatly, he took it back to the table.

The book dealt with the rise and fall of Nazi Germany.

The picture showed a meeting in a forest clearing between two uniformed men, each giving the Nazi salute. In the background were more men, some in uniform, some in civilian clothes, looking on respectfully. There were also, showing between the trees, some half-finished huts.

The caption was headed: PRELUDE TO DEATH. It went on, in smaller print:

Heinrich Himmler, head of the SS and Gestapo, pays a visit to the death camp at Grünberg as it nears completion. With him is the camp commandant, Gruppenführer Heinrich Mueller, soon to be known and dreaded as the Ghoul of Grünberg. (See pp. 305–7.)

Karen was not unfamiliar with Himmler's face. She had seen it often enough before, in books and magazines and on the TV screen, without paying it much attention. Now, however, she was struck by its almost reptilian weakness—the receding chin, the blind-looking eyes behind the small glasses under the high-crowned peaked hat. Only the hat itself seemed to have any forcefulness or strength. Without that hat and uniform, the all-powerful leader would have looked like an insignificant shoe-store clerk.

But if *he* looked insignificant, what of the younger man? He too wore a high hat, but his face was a complete blank as to character. Clean-shaved, with eyes that appeared to have neither lashes nor brows, and a slightly pouting mouth that looked neither vicious nor mild, he could have been anything: clerk, school-teacher, doctor, dentist, postman. He certainly bore little resemblance to Dr. Mendelssohn—except perhaps for his height. On the other hand, it wasn't impossible to imagine him, fleshed-out and forty years older, *as* Mendelssohn.

"Usually they *were* very nondescript little men, the top Nazis," said Irma, as if reading Karen's thoughts. "Probably that's why they became such beasts when they did get hold of power. Taking their revenge for being snubbed and overlooked earlier in their lives. You have only to compare the faces of those two with the men opposite."

This showed pictures of two regular German Army generals: Field Marshal Rommel and General Guderian.

"Tough, yes," said Irma. "Ruthless, certainly. But only in the way soldiers have to be. Even ours. But at least they were real men. Not," she said, turning back to the opposite page, "psychopathic sewer rats like these!"

Karen felt somewhat relieved. After all, she had German blood in her veins, too.

"We all have our gangsters and murderers, I guess," she said, quietly.

Gideon's final move was to take this book to the copying machine and have copies made of the death-camp picture. He seemed very concerned to get the clearest possible reproduction, making several reductions and enlargements.

"To refresh his memory," said Irma. "Next time he sees Mendelssohn. I told you he is thorough."

Danny had had the easiest time.

He was already at the cemetery when Joe and Carlos arrived.

It had been another sunny day, but a lot less warm. The sky had started to cloud over, and there were fewer people around. Even the bird-feeding lady hadn't shown.

"Is Grogan anywhere around?" was Joe's first question.

"Forget him," said Danny. "He had to go to Hartford to give evidence in a trial. He spent most of the morning in his office going over his notes and papers. He won't be bothering Gideon today."

Just then, Gideon strolled into the cemetery, carrying a plastic bag. Not far behind him, Karen and Irma followed.

"What's he got there, I wonder?" said Joe.

"Sunflower seeds," said Carlos, who'd darted forward to read the label.

"Now that's what I call smart!" said Joe as Gideon sat on one of the benches and started tossing the seeds onto the ground. "It gives him a reason for sitting here on a cold day, if anyone happens to look his way. . . . Hi, Karen! Hi, Irma! I was just admiring this guy's style."

"You don't know *anything* yet!" said Karen. "Wait until we tell you what he's been doing today."

"So go ahead," said Joe.

The girls briefly reported what they had seen and heard. Oblivious to this, the subject of their report went on feeding the birds. He seemed to enjoy it, too. His face lit up when he managed to get a chickadee to snatch a seed he'd placed at the other end of the bench.

"He looks like just another bird nut!" said Karen, smiling, when they'd brought the others up to date. "Anyway, how about you guys?"

"Don't even ask!" groaned Carlos.

Wacko and Buzz were just arriving.

"We'll tell you later," said Joe.

The meeting was very brief, this time. Taking his

cue from the man's casual demeanor, Buzz nodded and said, "Nice afternoon!"

"Yes," said Gideon, shivering, "if you are a polar bear! Does the weather always change so suddenly here?"

"There's a saying in these parts," said Buzz, sitting down, "that if you don't like the weather, stick around for five minutes, and it'll be sure to change."

"Doesn't it change so quickly where you come from?" Wacko said, with slightly narrowed eyes.

"Hey! Hear that?" said Carlos. "That's my Wacko! That's the lawyer's son!"

Gideon didn't even blink as he replied.

"In big cities you rarely notice these things. . . . Here. Take a handful each. Feed the birds. Look like that's all you're interested in. But tell me about your decision."

"We'll help you all we can," said Buzz.

Gideon flashed Wacko a look.

"You, too?"

"Of course. If the guy is the Ghoul of Grünberg, we'd be jerks not to."

"Splendid!" said Gideon, in a voice so low he might have been praising the chickadee for the way it was prying a seed open. "With your help we can crack this case."

"By the way," said Buzz. "We'd better warn you right away. Don't underestimate Detective Grogan."

Karen gasped.

Joe muttered, "Idiot!" and reached out to touch Buzz's lip. "You're not supposed to know about that!"

Gideon had stopped short, his hand in the seed bag. Then he relaxed.

"I suppose your father mentioned it," he said, giving Wacko a grin. "Well, thanks for the tip. Actually, I never underestimate professionals—especially policemen." He tossed a handful of seeds at some sparrows and offered the bag to the boys again. "Have you gleaned anything new about Camp Wednesday?"

The boys shook their heads.

"No," said Gideon. "I suppose it's early yet. But you will keep trying?"

"You bet!" said Buzz, while Wacko nodded vigorously.

"Good. Well, the moment you do, give me a call—"

"Lakeview Hotel, right?" said Wacko.

"Aw, *Wacko!*" groaned Carlos, reaching out to touch his lip. "Don't *you* start getting careless!"

But he needn't have worried. Once again, Gideon had stiffened. And once again he quickly relaxed.

"Of course—your father and Mr. Grogan. I was wondering how you knew where I was staying. . . . Yes. Call me there, but do *not* give your report. Just say, 'Aunt Gerda was inquiring about you—' and I'll get back to you on a safer line as soon as possible."

He stood up, crumpling the empty bag.

Then he gave one further proof of his absolute top quality as an agent.

"By the way," he said, giving Wacko a quick impish grin, "you didn't tell me you'd once visited Camp Wednesday yourself!"

More than Buzz and Wacko looked startled then.

"Yes," said Wacko. "But—but only for an hour or two."

Gideon laughed.

"Yes. At the camp's At-Home Day, last year, right? You went with your old friend, the poor little chap who got himself electrocuted."

"Hey! How does he know *that?*" the "poor little chap" yelped.

They all shook their heads. Karen and Irma looked at each other, mystified.

Buzz asked Gideon the same question. Gideon smiled.

"It's OK. Nothing sinister. I happened to be looking over some back issues of the *Journal*. There was a picture of you both in the computer room."

"Oh—yes . . ."

Wacko looked satisfied. Karen didn't.

"Hey, now wait a minute! Wacko's face didn't come out at all clearly, did it, Irma?"

But Irma was smiling.

"No. But Carlos's was very clear."

"Yeah!" said Carlos. "But he's never seen *me!*"

"He's seen a photograph," said Irma. "Probably back in Jerusalem."

"In—?" Carlos looked staggered. "*Me? My* picture?"

"Yes. When he was being briefed. When it was realized that the key to this inquiry would be Buzz, there'd be very careful inquiries made about his family and special friends. And the special friends of his

104

special friends." Irma shrugged. "If all that information hadn't already been collected, you can be sure that Gideon lost no time in gathering it when he arrived here."

"Wow!" said Karen. "Now that *is* thorough!"

"As I told you earlier," said Irma, "and as I am telling you all now, if those two boys"—she nodded toward Buzz and Wacko as they left the cemetery, not far behind the man—"can give Gideon something really concrete to work on, I wouldn't give one of those sunflower-seed shells for the chances of Mueller and Schmidt escaping justice!"

"Let's see that they do have something concrete to give him then!" said Joe. "Karen, Irma—keep after Gideon. You others come with me. We'll meet up again at the Lakeview Hotel, later."

15
The Place Haunter Remembers

When they arrived at the Lakeview Hotel, a couple of hours later, Joe, Carlos and Danny were surprised to see Gideon going in through the revolving door.

"Hey! Don't tell me he's only just arrived!" said Carlos, alarmed. He'd just spent another fruitless half hour looking for the bug, after they'd made their report and discussed the latest developments with the boys.

"Don't worry!" said Karen, who'd been waiting in the parking lot with Irma. "He'd only slipped out to make a call from the gas station."

"A call to Buzz," said Irma.

"How'd you know that?" said Danny.

"We listened to Gideon's side of the conversation, of course," said Karen. "It was about our suspicion that Wolfgang might be blackmailing Mendelssohn."

"Buzz must have called him right after we left," said Joe. "Good kid! . . . Well, how did Gideon react to *that?*"

"Very interested," said Irma. "As I knew he would be. He said if it were true, then there was a gap between the two men that could be widened into a major split."

"And then everything would come spilling out," said Karen.

"Did he say *how* it could be widened?" said Joe.

"No." Irma shook her head. "I imagine he was thinking of some form of needling. Something to stir up trouble between the two men."

"Hm!" Joe murmured. Then he changed the subject. "Did he ask Buzz how they knew about this?"

Karen grinned.

"Yes. But Buzz must have stalled, because Gideon ended by saying, 'All right, all right! Just so long as you yourselves feel it is information that can be relied upon!' "

"Well," said Joe, "it's hardly concrete evidence, but at least it's something for Gideon to be mulling over. Meanwhile, let's see if we can get lucky with that place-haunting lady on 106."

They found her gazing at the darkened terraces of her rose garden.

"Good evening," said Karen.

The woman was startled. A tremor of fear crossed her fat, sad features when she saw that the girls were accompanied by three males.

"What—what do you want?"

"We're sorry to disturb you," said Irma, smiling her special reassuring flight-attendant's smile. "But we were telling our friends what a lovely place this is, and they said they'd like to see it for themselves."

"Oh—yes . . ." The woman seemed less uneasy. "Yes, it is, isn't it?"

"Nice house," said Joe, looking up at the building.

The glow from a lighted window fell on the words ARMSTRONG CONSTRUCTION, lending authority to his comment. The woman's face relaxed further.

"Yes," she said. "A beautiful house."

"Beautful gardens, too," said Karen.

The woman sighed.

"You should see them in spring and summer!"

"The people here must take good care of them," said Joe.

"The people here are creeps!" said the woman.

"Oh?" Joe looked up. "They don't seem—"

"What do *you* know?" snapped the woman. "Only I know what they're really like. And I know they're creeps!"

"If you say so, ma'am."

"I do say so! That smirking lout in the kitchen there, pouring himself another drink—he's my nephew. That's his wife, just passing behind him. I know them only too well—*now!*"

She spit out the last word.

"You mean—?"

"I mean they promised me, before I—before I became what I am now—that they would take care of this place—*cherish* it—as good as I did for over forty years. And like a fool I believed them. And they even promised me again, on my very deathbed." She groaned. "Oh, if only I'd had it written into the will!"

"You see," said Karen, addressing Joe as if this were all new to him, "they're planning to sell the property to Dr. Mendelssohn. To do what he likes with."

"That's right," moaned the woman. Then she checked herself. "How do *you* know?"

"You told us. Last night."

"Oh, yes. . . . I'd forgotten."

This caused some of the visitors to look despairing. But Joe pressed on.

"We might be able to help you, ma'am. If *you* can help us."

The woman's eyes widened momentarily. Then the hope was displaced by a look of scornful pessimism.

"Huh! How? How can *you* help? I can't even get through to them myself, and I've been trying night and day—ever since the camp people made their first inquiries and these two started nibbling. That Mendelssohn guy is patient, I'll say that. He's pretended not to be all that interested. But he's been raising the offer slowly but surely, and now he only has to up it another twenty thousand, and they'll clinch it. I've heard them say so."

Joe had been nodding.

"I wasn't thinking of getting through to *them*, ma'am. I was—well, listen. Suppose it turned out that Dr. Mendelssohn is a murderer. That he'd killed one of the campers and concealed the body. If that came out, it would be enough to have the camp closed down, wouldn't it?"

She gaped.

"Are you telling me that this has really happened?"

"We think so. But let me finish. If Mendelssohn was jailed and the camp was closed down, why, then— the deal would be off. Permanently."

Her eyes shone.

"Gee! And would I love to see the looks on the faces of those two, *then!* . . ." Then she shook her head. "But no. You must be joking."

"Believe me, ma'am, I was never more serious in all my—I was never more serious!"

"And you think I can help?"

"Maybe. The name of the camper was David Rafferty. We think he was killed last year, early July—"

"Ah! The roses in early July!"

"Ma'am?"

"Sorry. Go on."

"He was sixteen—tall for his age, thin, with a bony look about his face. He had wiry red hair—"

"But why are you telling me this?" said the woman. "What am I supposed—?"

"We wondered if you'd seen him hanging around. Since. His ghost."

The woman shivered slightly.

"I can't say I have. No . . . I don't go wandering around *that* place, you know."

"No. But *he* may have wandered around *here*."

She shook her head again.

"What difference would it make, anyway?"

"If we could trace him, he'd be able to tell us where they'd buried him—his body. And then—"

"And then *what*? What could *you* do about it?"

"Maybe get through to the police, ma'am," said Joe. "Through some living person. Like someone holding a séance or something."

The woman's eyes stayed wide, this time.

"Is—is that *possible?*"

"Well, David's parents have hired an investigator. And if the investigator can't come up with anything the usual way, we know he'd be willing to bring in a psychic—a pair of psychics. Then we might have a chance."

The woman sighed.

"I wish you luck. I really do. But I can't say that I've seen anyone answering that description. . . . Mind you"—her eyes narrowed—"there *was* a man who mentioned something weird . . . some . . . some sort of strange goings-on over there."

They all went very still.

"In Camp Wednesday, ma'am?"

"Yes. . . . But I can't remember the details. I wasn't paying much attention, I guess. Anyway, he was sort of distressed about his own affairs. And I don't think he'd paid it all that much attention himself."

"When was this?"

"Oh, around the time you mentioned. That was the summer these creeps started cutting down on the time they spent over the roses. I mean, can you imagine? All those aphids and—"

"Yes, ma'am," said Joe. "They really are a couple of jerks. Let's hope we can spoil their plans."

"You bet!" said the woman.

"So this guy—I guess he was a ghost himself—"

"Yes. I mean how could I have spoken with him, otherwise?"

"Sure. Do you remember anything else about him? Is he still around?"

"Well, no. He was only at the camp for a week or two. While it was in session. He'd come to—yes!—now I'm beginning to remember—he'd come to try and make contact with his son."

"Really? Why?"

"Oh, the usual! The son had been feeling depressed, talking suicide, blaming himself for his father's death. Mistakenly, it seems. I wasn't listening too closely. He'd started me wondering if the roses ever blamed themselves for making me work too hard at them, when the doctor said I should get all the rest I could . . ."

She fell silent. Joe waited, then said: "This guy, ma'am? And his son? Do you recall—"

"I only saw him that one time. The day his son quit the camp."

"Before the end of the session?"

"Yes. The man said he wasn't sorry, either. The kid's mother had sent him there, thinking it would take his mind off his troubles. But it didn't. And that German doctor was giving him a hard time, the father said. Telling the kid to snap out of it, and be a man, and stop sniveling, and stuff. *He* sounds like a jerk, too. Did you say he was actually a murderer?"

"We believe so. But you were saying . . . the father wasn't sorry."

"That's what he told me. He said there were some peculiar things going on in there. Especially after lights-out. He said he'd seen some kind of weird ritual. A—hey, yes!—*like a burial!*"

Something like a charge of electricity went through the five visitors.

Joe had trouble controlling his voice.

"What—what kind of burial, ma'am? Where?"

"Gee!" The woman looked vexed. "I wish I'd paid more attention now! I figured he'd seen some kind of initiation rite. You know what kids are like. And, being so upset about his son already, he'd made too much out of it. That's what I figured."

"And you can't remember anything else? Any details?"

"Sorry. No. I just lost interest."

"What about *him?* The guy himself?"

"Well . . ." The woman frowned. "He—he came from someplace local. I do know that."

"Did he say where?"

"No. I just figured he did. He said he was on his way back home, to be close to the kid again. I asked him how he was going to get there, and he said that was no problem. He could walk it in under an hour. He'd been taking a shortcut through here, in fact."

Karen was looking excited.

"A son, sixteen or seventeen? Ma'am—did he tell you his name?"

"Yes. But I've forgotten it. Probably forgot it as soon as he said it. All I remember is that it began with a *Q*. Like my favorite rosebush of all, the Queen Elizabeth over there. Which," she added, scowling, "should be covered with burlap by this time. Before the cold really begins to bite . . ."

But now *they* weren't listening.

Danny had said, "Hey! That might be Andy Quigley! His father did die in some kind of road accident, about a couple of years ago."

"You're right!" said Karen. "And he was very upset. He was a classmate of mine and—"

"Do you know where he lives?" said Joe, looking tense.

"Sure!" said Danny. "*I* do. I used to deliver papers there. It's on the other side of town."

"I wonder whether his father's still around," muttered Joe. Then he clapped his hands. "We'd better check right away. This could be the breakthrough we've been looking for!"

16
Concrete Evidence

They reached the Quigley house just after midnight. It was in darkness—like most of the other small ranch houses nearby.

"I hope Andy's getting over his depression," said Karen. "But I also hope that Mr. Quigley's still around."

It didn't look like it. There was nobody at all to be seen as they prowled around the single-story building.

"Maybe he's inside," said Joe.

He started calling Mr. Quigley's name, softly at first, then louder, with his head close to one of the windows. The others followed suit, going from window to window, their urgent voices merging and echoing.

"Mr. Quigley . . . igley . . . igleee!"

There was no reply from inside. But then, after a few minutes, they heard a groan.

115

"What was that?" said Irma.

"It seemed to come from in there," said Danny, pointing to the garage.

"Are you sure?" said Joe, going up to the garage door. "I—"

He broke off when he heard the muttering.

"Who would be calling for *me?* Doesn't everyone know I'm dead? I must have imagined it. . . ."

The voice sounded weary, tremulous.

"Mr. Quigley," said Joe. "Is that you?"

Dead silence.

Then, very cautiously, the reply.

"Who wants to know?"

"Some friends of Andy's," said Karen. "We went to the same school."

"You—you mean you're—like me?"

"Ghosts," said Karen. "Yes."

"Listen," came the voice, less weary but still guarded. "Around the back there's a window. It's slightly open. We'll be able to talk better there."

The window was dirty. All they were able to see was a dim shape, standing there. The man really did look ghostly, Danny thought, trying to make out the features of his old newspaper customer. The situation was getting to be like a regular séance.

"What do you want from me?" said the shape.

"We may be able to help you," said Joe.

"No one can help me!" groaned the man.

"We may be able to help *Andy*," insisted Joe.

Another groan.

"It's beginning to look like no one can help him, either!"

"Just tell us your problem," said Joe. "And we'll see."

"Well . . . OK," came the despondent reply.

Danny had been right. Mr. Quigley had been killed in a road accident. A single-car accident. There had been something wrong with the car's steering, and he'd lost control going down a winding slope.

The trouble was—and here the man's voice nearly choked up—he had known about the fault.

"I'd noticed it. A few days previously. I—I was on my way from Poughkeepsie. I stopped by at a garage. The guy gave it a test drive. Said it was some intermittency in the cable. That's why it wasn't faulty all the time. It kept righting itself. He suggested I leave the car there and borrow another. But—it was miles from home. I decided to risk it and go very slowly. It was late when I reached here. The others had gone to bed. Next morning, we visited my wife's brother, over in Greenwich. We went in her car—we usually did on weekends. Andy stayed home."

From then on, the story came out punctuated with sobs. The dim shape seemed to crumple.

Andy, unknown to his parents, had borrowed his father's car that evening. He too had had trouble with the steering. But because he hadn't had permission, he didn't dare mention the fault right away. When his father took the car out the next day, it was too late.

"In fact, it had slipped my mind altogether," said Mr. Quigley. "It seemed to behave perfectly. Then, suddenly—the steering went."

Andy had blamed himself. If only he'd had the

sense—and the courage—to report the fault immediately, his father would never have been killed.

The visitors looked at each other. It was a familiar story. The trouble was, it seemed that you could only see such misunderstandings for what they were when you were a ghost. And by then it was usually too late.

Not in this case, though.

"Do you think we *can* help, Joe?" whispered Karen.

"It shouldn't be difficult," said Carlos. "If we had the name of the garage, Buzz or Wacko could give them a call and ask them to explain to Mrs. Quigley and Andy that Mr. Quigley knew about the fault already."

"Leave it to me," said Joe, going back to the window. "Mr. Quigley—can you tell me the name of the garage?"

The dim shape seemed to pull itself together.

"Sure! Sonny's. On Route 55. The guy logged that test drive in his book. If only Andy could get to see it! But—it was too far away. They must never have heard about the crash. So nobody got in touch. I've tried—heaven knows!"

"Take it easy, Mr. Quigley," Joe said. "I think we may be able to help. . . ."

Then he spoke—very cautiously—about their occasional ability to contact the living. Again he made it appear to have something to do with clairvoyance.

"Really?" said the man. "You really think you can do it? Oh, how can I ever thank you enough? How—?"

"Like this," said Joe. "You can try to remember the

time Andy went to Camp Wednesday. That ritual burial. Remember?"

"Sure! Of course!"

The possibility of getting some real help for Andy seemed to have done wonders for the man's memory. Without even asking why they wanted to know, or who had told them about the incident in the first place, he proceeded to tell them everything he had seen and heard.

"Well," he began, "I don't suppose it really *was* a body, but it was roughly that size and shape, wrapped in black plastic. All trussed up.

"Anyway, it was being carried by these two guys. One of them was the camp director—some German guy—and the other was German, too. I know that because when they spoke, mainly in whispers, sometimes it would be in German."

"Do you know any German?" asked Karen.

"Only enough to recognize it as German. . . . Anyway, like I was saying, these two came down past the tennis courts, in the middle of the night, carrying this—this object. And—well—at first I thought it might be a corpse, at that. And since my kid was staying at that camp, I thought I'd better find out more. Just anxiety, really. Because even if it had been a body—well, what could *I* have done?"

"Did you definitely find out it wasn't a body then?" said Irma.

"Well, no. But come on! Directors of summer camps don't usually go around burying stiffs in the middle of the night, do they? And—well—there was the circumstantial evidence."

"What circumstantial evidence?" said Joe.

"The place they buried it. You see, when they reached the lake, they took it over the bridge—a temporary bridge, fixed by the contractors working on the island. And that's where they buried it. On the island. In the hole the contractor had prepared for the concrete base of the statue. They were fairly careful about placing it, dead center, and covering it with the earth and sand or whatever it was the contractor was using at the bottom, ready for pouring in the concrete. I tell you, it gave me the willies, seeing them working down there, so furtively."

"So you still thought it might be a body?" said Irma.

"Sure. But it was the following day when the truth dawned. When the chief contractor noticed there'd been a disturbance down in the hole. The other German was with him, and he told the guy not to be so fussy. Then the guy got mad. He said he was sure some campers had been fooling around and he wasn't going to pour any concrete in until it had been checked out. Then the director came and said it was OK. All it was, was a time capsule. He said the job was already far behind schedule. He said the contractor had better start pouring or he might find himself having to wait for his money."

"What's a time capsule?" said Danny.

"A bundle of newspapers, records, cans of Coke, stuff like that," said Carlos. "So that when people dig it up in a couple of centuries, they'll get some idea how people lived in these times."

"Yes. That's roughly how the director explained it," said Mr. Quigley. "But it only seemed to get the contractor madder. He started roaring about gimmicks, saying no gimmick like that was going to be allowed to spoil one of *his* jobs. But they gradually got him to calm down. The director offered him an extra bonus—in cash, tax-free—if he'd get on with the pouring."

"Angus MacGregor!"

They all stared at Joe.

"Excuse me?" said Mr. Quigley.

"Angus MacGregor. He was the contractor. And now *I* remember, too," said Joe, turning to the others. "Angus was still sore about it, the night I heard him sounding off outside the Shamrock Bar. I wonder . . ."

His face clouded as he trailed off.

Then he shook his head and turned.

"Mr. Quigley, can you recall where they brought the—the bundle *from?*"

"Somewhere up the hill. The house, probably. Director's Residence. Hey—and yes! That was another thing that gave me the creeps!"

"What?"

"Well, I say it gave me the creeps, but to be honest I've never given it any thought since—being so worried about Andy. But there was a scream, a few nights earlier. From up there."

"The director's house?"

"Yes. That was very late, too. At first I thought it was somebody in terrible pain."

"It wasn't—not an owl?" asked Irma.

"No. No way. That was a human scream, all right! But there was nothing after that. So I guessed it was probably a late-late movie, and somebody had turned the sound up momentarily when they'd meant to turn it down. I mean, there was a dim light, with the flicker of a TV screen, behind the drapes in one room."

The visitors remained silent for a few seconds. They knew only too well that their search was over.

"Art, Science and Youth!" murmured Carlos.

"What?" said Mr. Quigley.

"Name of the statue. And now we can put a name to that 'Youth.' "

"Poor devil!" Irma added, in a whisper, her eyes squeezed shut, with a deep line of pain between them.

Joe turned to the window.

"Mr. Quigley," he said, "thank you very much. Believe me, we'll do everything in our power to get that information through to some living person."

"You mean the information about the garage?"

"That too. Yes. Then a simple phone call should be enough to clear everything up."

"You don't know what this means to me!" said the man as they began to move off.

"I think we do," said Karen, giving him a sad smile. "You're very lucky, Mr. Quigley!"

Then she ran to catch up with the others, in time to hear Joe saying, "So there's our concrete evidence. Now we can let Gideon know exactly where David is buried." He gave a twisted smile. "*Concrete* is the right word, too. *Under* concrete. Several *tons* of concrete!"

17
Buzz's Great Idea

The strain of waiting to pass on this vital new information might have proved too much for even the more patient members of the squad. Fortunately, the next day was Saturday, and Joe had already scheduled their next meeting with Buzz and Wacko for 8:30 A.M.

Even so, Carlos was so fizzing with excitement as he stood in front of the word processor, flexing his fingers, that Joe had to caution him.

"Easy, Carlos! Don't flip *now*, for Pete's sake!"

Danny closed his eyes, not daring to look.

Carlos nodded and took a deep breath.

Then his fingers went into action, stabbing out the message that had Buzz and Wacko rising from their seats.

"*We now know where David Rafferty is buried! Repeat: We now know where David Rafferty is buried! Pay closest attention. . . .*"

123

There was no need for that last admonition. Buzz and Wacko couldn't have been more alert as they sank back on their chairs, absorbing every flickering word that followed.

"So—" Buzz began, when the report was neatly but excitedly rounded off with a row of exclamation points.

"Write!!"

Sorry! Buzz scribbled on his pad. *So now we call Gideon and tell him where the body is. Right?*

"Right!"

Will do, wrote Buzz, his eyes gleaming.

Then Wacko moved to the word processor.

"Shall we tell him also about Angus MacGregor? Maybe if Gideon got in touch with him, he'd gather some useful corroborative evidence."

"Impossible!" came the reply.

Wacko frowned. Buzz scribbled, *Why?*

Carlos turned to Joe. Joe shrugged.

"You might as well tell them."

Other members of the Ghost Squad had made the same suggestion, hours earlier, and Joe had shaken his head, his face clouding again.

"No use. Angus MacGregor was drowned, a few nights after I'd overheard him raising Cain. In fact, now that I come to think of it, that's just what he did do. Raise Cain."

"Cain?"

"Cain was a murderer, remember."

"What happened? To Angus?"

"Well, he was walking home from that same bar— drunk, as usual. He lived nearby, down by the river,

124

you know. . . . And on this particular night he missed his footing on the riverbank. People always said Angus would end like that, one day."

"Well—obviously they were right," Karen had said.

"Right, nothing! When I was living, I used to see Angus all the time, on one construction site or another. Angus the Mountain Goat, we used to call him. I've seen him myself, moving around on girders six inches wide and one hundred feet up. With a skinful of liquor. Now if he'd fallen to his death *that* route, I'd have thought he'd run out of luck at last. But not from a riverside path!" At this point, Joe had groaned. "Why, oh why, didn't I think of this before? The first time we rode around Camp Wednesday?"

"You think he was murdered?"

"I'm *sure* of it, Danny! Can't you imagine how uneasy they'd be, wondering if Angus would ever get wise to them? Can't you imagine Mueller being determined to rub him out, the first opportunity? Especially when it got back to them that Angus was still sounding off about the concrete bed?"

When Carlos had finished passing on this information, Buzz wrote, *Is Angus's ghost around?*

"Not as far as we know. Why?"

Buzz was grinning.

Well, maybe we can make those two guys believe they're being haunted by two *of their victims,* he scribbled. *Not just one!*

Wacko looked puzzled. So did the three ghosts.

"Has he gone out of his mind?" said Carlos.

"Sure looks like it!" said Danny.

"Ask him what he means," snapped Joe. "Tell him this is no laughing matter."

Buzz shook his head when he read the message.

No. I'm deadly serious, he wrote. *What I had in mind was . . .*

He filled three pages with his explanation. And, as it unfolded, Joe's look of annoyance was replaced by one of admiration—and grins began to appear on some of the others' faces.

After letting Gideon know these new facts, the Ghost Squad doesn't have to just sit on its hands. We could do a beautiful number on Mendelssohn and Wolfgang. Get them so rattled they'll make all kinds of mistakes. And this is how. After I call Gideon, I also call Mendelssohn. I speak in a faraway sort of voice, like you guys are supposed to use. I say I am David Rafferty, come out from under the statue to haunt them. That in itself should shake them rigid—the fact that, even if it's a spoof, someone out there knows the exact location of the body. But that isn't all. I say that to prove I really am a ghost, I shall keep touching them on their noses. That, sure, all they will feel is a faint, cool, brushing sensation—but they'd better believe it is me, David Rafferty. Naturally, you guys will have to do the actual touching. But—well, how about it?

Carlos was jumping with glee. Danny's face was glowing. Joe laughed out loud.

"Tell him," he said, "tell him that's the best idea I've heard in a long while! But—wait—tell him to hold the call to Mendelssohn until 10:30."

"Oh, but *why?*" said Carlos.

"So that hopefully we'll have time to collect Karen and Irma and get up to Camp Wednesday, ready to see the effect of the call for ourselves. Also to follow through immediately. Hey—and tell them we'll be back here at one o'clock to report the results. They should be something else—they really should!"

18
The Chain Boost

"Buzz didn't lose any time calling *that* one in!" said Karen, when Joe, Danny and Carlos arrived at the Lakeview Hotel's front lot.

"Gideon's been given the message, then?" said Joe.

"Ten minutes ago," said Irma.

"Where is he now?" said Joe.

"Back inside the hotel," said Karen. "He was looking very thoughtful."

"I'll bet he was!" said Carlos. "Did he ask how Buzz knew?"

"No," said Irma. "He was obviously too absorbed by the news itself."

"Did Buzz tell him about his own idea?" said Danny.

"Of course not!" said Joe. "That *would* have blown our secret!"

"What idea?" asked Karen.

When Joe had finished explaining, the girls' reactions were the same as the other three's had been.

"Hey! Wow! What a dilly!" cried Karen.

Irma's eyes had an eager gleam as she laughed and said, "We can even use the Chain Boost!"

"Chain Boost?" said Joe. "What's that?"

"Don't you call it that over here?" said Irma. "When two or more ghosts hold hands before touching a living person?"

They stared at her.

"Go on," said Joe. "What happens?"

Irma laughed.

"You mean you don't know? Why, the touch becomes more noticeable."

Carlos's eyes had widened.

"Hey! Like batteries? If two of us link up, it will double the charge? And three—?"

"Well, no. It doesn't seem to go up in proportion. But it does increase it *somewhat*. And there are limits. After four or five join up, there is no increase at all. . . . But let me show you. Join hands now and come over here."

Irma led them to a car where a man and woman were loading their baggage. The man was putting a suitcase in the trunk. The woman was opening one of the rear doors, a vanity case in her hand.

"Now!" said Irma, joining hands with Karen, who was already linked with Carlos, Danny and Joe.

Irma touched the woman on the ear.

"*Hey!*" The woman spun around. "Cut it out!"

"Huh?" The man looked up. "Cut what out?"

"Touching me with an ice-cold finger!"

"What ice-cold finger?" said the man, lifting his gloved hands.

"Oh—" The woman blinked, looked up, shivered.

"I guess it must have been a stray snowflake," said the man.

"Mighty big snowflake! Besides, it isn't snowing."

"Not *yet*," said the man, glancing at the blue gray sky. "But it isn't far off. Probably a forerunner."

The ghosts were already moving off, doubly eager now to get to Camp Wednesday.

When they reached the Director's Residence, it was only 10:15 by the clock in a blue Porsche parked at the door.

"But suppose we can't get inside the house?" said Carlos.

"We'll just have to wait until we can," said Joe.

"Yeah, but I'd love to see their faces when they get Buzz's message!"

"At least they're both home," said Danny, coming away from the window of the big room.

"Someone's coming now," said Irma, pointing to the door.

It was Wolfgang, with the dog. The ghosts moved forward, but Wolfgang had let the dog out and shut the storm door again before any of them could slip through.

Carlos groaned.

"Wait," said Joe, grinning. "It won't be long before he opens it again."

The dog had trotted to a bush and was cocking its

leg. Wolfgang was watching from behind the storm door. The dog turned, sniffed the air, then began to walk back. Wolfgang opened the door. The dog paused to sniff at one of the car's wheels.

"Prinz!" snapped Wolfgang.

The dog was obedient. Too obedient. Only Carlos and Irma had managed to slip through before the dog was on the doorstep.

"Quick!" Irma grabbed Carlos's hand and touched Wolfgang's forehead.

Wolfgang paused with the door half-closed. He stared at the lintel, brushing his forehead with the back of his hand.

"Something wrong?"

Mendelssohn had come into the hall. Wolfgang was now feeling the lintel.

"No. It is just that I could swear I felt a drop of water."

Mendelssohn smiled.

"We are getting old, *mein Herr!* A trick of the old tired nerves."

Wolfgang flashed him an angry glance.

"*Ach!* Speak for yourself!"

The last couple of remarks had been in German. But Karen had plenty of time to translate, now that they were all safely inside.

"Oh, boy!" said Carlos. "Trick of the nerves, huh? They ain't felt *nothin'* yet!" He turned to the phone in the hall. "Come on, Buzz! Come on, come on!"

The minute hand of the grandfather's clock was just approaching 10:30.

Mendelssohn, Wolfgang and the dog were going into the room.

"We'd better follow them," said Joe. "There's a phone in there, too."

They hurried in unnecessarily. Neither man bothered to close the door.

"I was wondering," Mendelssohn said, speaking his softly accented English again, "if you would—"

The phone rang. The ghosts started. Only the men and the dog seemed relaxed. Mendelssohn picked up the phone and said, "Yes?"

Only then did a slight frown crease his forehead.

"This is he, yes. . . ." Then the crease seemed to leap as it deepened. "*Who?*"

His face was turning gray. Wolfgang took one look and headed for the hall. They heard him lift the receiver out there.

"It's Buzz!" Carlos cried gleefully, getting his ear as close as he could to the instrument Mendelssohn was holding.

"But—but—is this—is this—?"

Mendelssohn's hand was beginning to tremble alarmingly.

Wolfgang snapped out a command from the hall, his hand over the mouthpiece.

" 'Be quiet and listen!' " Karen translated.

Still trembling, Mendelssohn fell silent. The ghosts crowded closer. Mendelssohn seemed scared even of the receiver, holding it a dithering half inch from his ear.

So they all managed to catch something of Buzz's

132

message—more or less as he'd outlined it earlier. He seemed to be relishing the part of David Rafferty's ghost, letting his words rise and fall and fade and come back again—before suddenly wailing into song.

" 'Should auld acquaintance be forgot . . .' " Then a throaty chuckle. Then: "You know who I learned that from, Mendelssohn? Another old friend of yours. Angus MacGregor . . . Yes, *that* made you gasp, didn't it? Poor Angus MacGregor! Oh, yes! He's around someplace, too. Weeds and mud sticking to him, weeds and mud from the bottom of the river. Maybe *he'll* be after your noses, too. Maybe not. But *I* will, Mendelssohn. And very soon . . . very . . . very . . . soooon!"

There was a click.

"Wow!" gasped Carlos, awed. "I hope he didn't overdo it!"

"Mendelssohn didn't think so," said Karen. "Look at him!"

The camp director had slumped on a chair, clutching his heart. Beads of perspiration stood out on his forehead. His trembling lips were blue.

"Pull yourself together!" snapped Wolfgang, in English, stalking back into the room.

His face, too, had turned a pasty shade. But there was no trembling in his lips—drawn back from the crooked teeth in a snarl.

"But—but"—Mendelssohn waved feebly toward the phone—"didn't you—didn't you *hear?*"

"I heard!"

"Well—"

"It was a trick! It must have been!"

"It—*aieeow!*"

Mendelssohn shrieked, clutching his nose. The ghosts had made their first strike—a full five-ghost-power strike.

"Stop it! Immediately! You hysterical fool!"

Wolfgang had lifted his hand, ready to slap the other's face.

But it never got that far.

Instead, he felt at his nose—the cold eyes widening.

"You—you, too?" quavered Mendelssohn.

The dog whimpered inquiringly as it gazed up at Wolfgang.

"There! Even Prinz!" gasped Mendelssohn. "Even the dog can sense—some—some presence!"

"Rubbish!" snapped Wolfgang—though he was now looking about him uneasily. "The dog is just wondering what the fuss is all about."

"No, no! Animals can tell. . . . And, besides . . . *I* felt it! *You* felt it!"

"We felt *something*," said Wolfgang, in a low voice. His eyes had a thoughtful gleam. "Some—some beam, some ray, maybe. Even lasers—who knows? We are not the only ones to have made electronic discoveries. And," he continued, in a slow grating voice, "it could very well be the work of that swine of a so-called siding salesman." He glanced down. "How do you feel now?" he asked, in a more considerate tone.

"Do you really think so, Wolfgang? That—that it's a trick?"

"It has to be! Where is your scientific sense—*Doctor* Mendelssohn?"

"So—?"

"So call him. Now. He is probably expecting us to. Well, we will not disappoint him. Let us take the initiative. Remember your training. 'When you are in a corner—' "

Wolfgang paused. The other's eyes were closed.

" 'When you are in a corner—hit back,' " he mumbled. "But Wolfgang—"

"Hit back *hard!* Hit back *fast!* The lightning backhand!"

The words in German seemed to have been spit out rather than spoken. Wolfgang's eyes were as hard as a snake's again.

"But—"

With an obvious effort, Wolfgang softened his tone as he interrupted.

"Just invite him. Play along with his insulation nonsense. Say we need his advice, after all. And right away. Tell him we have—uh—insulation problems. Mysterious drafts. Use that persuasive tongue of yours, Dr. Mendelssohn!"

As Karen translated and Mendelssohn fumbled through the telephone book for the Lakeview Hotel's number, the other ghosts were no longer laughing. They were beginning to wonder if Buzz's idea had been so great, after all.

"I do hope Gideon will be careful!" said Irma.

19
Wolfgang
Sets Another Trap

After making his call, Dr. Mendelssohn put down the phone and said, "Well, so be it. He will be around in about half an hour. I hope we are doing the right thing."

He was still pale. His eyes kept flitting about. But he was no longer trembling.

Wolfgang was hardly paying attention. He stood with his back to the fire, gazing at a spot high on the opposite wall—obviously thinking hard.

"One thing is clear, at any rate," he murmured. "MacGregor must have said something to someone before he died. Probably he'd guessed more than we realized he had."

Mendelssohn shrugged.

"That drunken sot! Who would take notice of anything *he* said?"

"No one, probably." Then Wolfgang scowled. "Until this—this Mishcon came along, jogging memories."

"You still think he is at the back of these—uh—the phone call?"

"I am convinced of it."

"But why?"

"I can think of many reasons. One hundred and fifty thousand reasons."

"Don't say that!"

Mendelssohn had shrunk back into his chair.

"Why not?" said Wolfgang, giving him a contemptuous glance. "It is probably the truth."

Mendelssohn had closed his eyes and clenched his fists, fighting to control the renewed trembling.

When it had subsided, he said, in a low shaky voice, "In that case—he will be sure to have some backup. They usually do."

"Not necessarily," drawled Wolfgang. "Not in the *early* stages of an investigation." He shrugged. "But if he does, we can always use him as a hostage."

Mendelssohn didn't seem impressed.

"And if not," he asked miserably, "what then?"

"We will allow ourselves a little more time. Set a very tempting trap. One in which he will regrettably be mistaken for an intruder." He flashed Mendelssohn a brief tusky smile. "We are two old men, are we not? Living alone? We have a right to protect ourselves. But our nerves are so worn and frail, we are only too likely to squeeze a trigger before we really mean to. Besides"— another smile—"there is always Prinz. . . . Excuse me, *Herr Doktor.*"

With a short bow that had much more mockery than respect in it, he left the room, with the Doberman at his heels.

The ghosts remained with Mendelssohn, anxious to get Karen's translation of the exchange, which had been entirely in German. When Karen had finished, Irma shook her head.

"If Gideon had realized that they had learned that *someone*, no matter who, now knows about David's burial place and Angus MacGregor's connection with it—well . . . He would never have agreed to come so soon. He would know it would be too dangerous."

"Why *did* he agree so soon, anyway?" said Karen.

"Oh, he probably believes they are suspicious of him *generally*. And he'll be prepared to risk another round of cat-and-mouse sparring. Especially if it gives him the opportunity to observe at firsthand some of the things we've told him. Like the blackmail possibility."

"But he definitely wouldn't come if he realized they knew their statue secret was out?" said Joe.

"Absolutely not."

Carlos began to fidget.

"Maybe we could get back to Wacko's and—"

"Too late," said Joe. "Gideon'll be on his way."

Mendelssohn had gotten up and was standing by the window. His hands were loosely clasped behind his back, but the fingers were twitching.

"We made a big mistake," said Danny. "Rushing in with Buzz's phone call like that. We got carried away. That's where impatience gets you," he said, giving Carlos an accusing look.

"You were just as eager as anyone else!"

Danny sighed. "I know."

Irma broke the ensuing silence.

"Another thing that worries me—"

Then she stopped. Like the others, she had heard the unmistakable sound of a car, crunching up the driveway.

"It was so good of you to come! Especially on a Saturday."

By some miracle of control, Dr. Mendelssohn seemed like his usual smiling self as he greeted the newcomer in the hall.

By another miracle of control, Gideon seemed like the eager smiling young salesman they'd seen before, as he shook hands with Mendelssohn.

"That's quite all right, sir. No trouble at all. Especially when there's a chance of new business." He looked around. "You say you have some—uh—strange drafts?"

"Yes," said Wolfgang. "Inexplicable drafts. Would you please follow me? I think they originate in the basement."

Smilingly, eagerly, Gideon followed Wolfgang and the dog down the stairs.

Not smilingly, Mendelssohn followed Gideon.

Wolfgang led them along a carpeted corridor.

"In here," he said, opening a door.

It was a sparsely furnished room. There was a plain table, some rickety-looking chairs, a pile of cartons. More like a junk room, really.

"This isn't where the TV monitors are, obviously," said Joe.

"No," said Carlos. He'd already gone to the window, half of which was above ground level. He glanced out at the driveway, where he could see Gideon's car, parked alongside the Porsche. "No bars. But it must be right next to the monitor room. I wish they'd show Gideon in *there!*"

"Be quiet!" said Joe.

The cat-and-mouse game was already in progress.

"As you will see," Wolfgang was saying, pointing to the window, "there is no double glazing in this room. Not even a storm window. Could that create drafts elsewhere in the house?"

Gideon frowned the frown of a young salesman trying to be helpful.

"It could, I suppose. In certain weather conditions. Especially if you leave the window like that."

It was open by about an inch, at the top.

"Even such a small crack?" said Wolfgang. "It could create narrow jets of cold air? Even upstairs?"

Gideon looked puzzled.

"Possibly." He glanced respectfully at Dr. Mendelssohn. "Why don't you have it closed anyway, sir?"

Mendelssohn blinked.

"I—Wolfgang looks after this kind of thing."

Wolfgang gave his curt mock-respectful bow and turned to Gideon.

"The catch is broken. I keep meaning to get a new one. It is too easy for intruders, like this."

"That's the trap!" said Irma. "He is hoping to tempt Gideon to break in, later. It is what Wolfgang must have come down to do, when he left the room."

Mendelssohn was nodding, after giving Wolfgang a quick approving glance.

"Yes. There is some very expensive electronic equipment in the next room. Very special."

"Very special indeed," drawled Wolfgang, watching Gideon's face. "We have been picking up some strange signals. A person claiming to be someone called MacGregor—his ghost. Right, Dr. Mendelssohn?"

Mendelssohn had been looking horrified. He pulled himself up with a jerk. "Well—yes. *Very* strange. Very disturbing."

Gideon had also been startled. It flashed across his face momentarily. He recovered even faster than Mendelssohn and grinned.

"But it is too late!" groaned Irma. "He showed it clearly. And Wolfgang *saw!*"

"Well, I doubt if Polinsulation can insulate a place against *ghosts!*" Gideon was saying, jokingly. "We may be able to screen out unwanted radio and TV interference, of course. Perhaps I could take a look in there?"

He turned, casually. But Wolfgang and the dog were between him and the door—and neither moved.

"He's stalling for time!" said Joe. "He's still fazed by that mention of MacGregor. He's probably wondering if they have some extraspecial eavesdropping equipment in there."

"Or if Buzz and Wacko have been on *their* side, all along!" said Irma.

"Hey!" protested Carlos. "What's that supposed to—?"

"Be quiet!" said Joe.

Mendelssohn was shaking his head.

"No—we can take care of radio interference ourselves."

"And any other kind of interference," said Wolfgang. He suddenly stiffened. "Mr. Mishcon," he snapped, "I must ask you not to open that case! Prinz! *Achtung!*"

The dog growled, showing its fangs. Its snout was pointing straight at Gideon's throat.

Gideon had frozen, one hand still on the catch of the briefcase.

"I was only going to show you one of our leaflets on TV and radio interference," he said, mildly.

"I am sure you were," drawled Wolfgang. "But Prinz is so—uh—paranoid. He suspects you may have a weapon in there." He put out a hand. "Permit me . . ."

"Of course," said Gideon, still smiling uncertainly, letting the man take the case from his hands.

"Oh, boy!" groaned Karen as Wolfgang began to open the case.

Wolfgang seemed surprised as he inspected the contents. There appeared to be nothing in there but leaflets, brochures and order forms.

"You say there is one on radio interference? . . . Ah—so there is."

Wolfgang looked disappointed.

"I told you Gideon was thorough!" said Irma, beginning to smile. "I—"

"Hello! What is *this*, Mr. Mishcon?"

Wolfgang was frowning now, as he picked up a piece of paper that had dropped from the leaflet.

The ghosts crowded closer. Irma gasped.

It was a picture of the Grünberg meeting between Himmler and Mueller, neatly clipped from the larger sheet of copy paper. Gideon's lips went very tight when he saw it. He had obviously—just this one time—not been thorough *enough*.

"Oh, *mein Gott!*" cried Mendelssohn, staring at it with wide terrified eyes.

Wolfgang remained very cool.

"Mr. Mishcon," he said, in a curious purring tone, "I think we had better go into this matter more thoroughly. I have some very serious questions to ask you. Which you will answer. . . . Permit me to escort you to the next room, where, among our special scientific instruments, there are some very sophisticated—" He clicked his tongue. "I was about to say 'lie detectors.' 'Truth extractors' would probably be more correct. And *please*—be very careful. One sudden jerky movement, and Prinz will be at your throat as fast as any bullet. And every bit as lethal."

"Quick, you guys!" said Joe. "Join hands!"

"Well," Wolfgang continued, "shall we go and—?"

Suddenly, Prinz's stiff alertness was transformed into a howling quivering. The dog gave a leap, another howl. Then another and another as Joe, at the end of the chain, kept prodding its nose.

Wolfgang and Mendelssohn were completely taken by surprise. After all, it was their own dog, and nothing like this had ever happened before.

Gideon was much quicker to react. As Wolfgang dived to grab the dog's collar and Mendelssohn dithered, the agent leaped for the door.

"Quick! Stop him!" Wolfgang yelled. "He's—"

That was when Prinz bit Wolfgang's forearm, pulling him up short, delaying pursuit for another few seconds. But he wasted no time on chastising the dog or even scolding it. Shaking it off, he ran from the room.

Trembling, Mendelssohn backed away from the dog and began to sidle toward the door.

"Good dog! You—*you* felt that touch, too, huh?"

Snarls were punctuating Prinz's whimpers already, as the dog looked around, showing the whites of its eyes.

Mendelssohn reached the door unbitten. He was probably hoping to shut the dog in. But Prinz, recovering fast now, perhaps reassured by Mendelssohn's tone, gave a sudden shake of the head, slipped past the man and went bounding off. Automatically, Mendelssohn shut the door behind him anyway.

"Hey!" yelled Carlos.

It had all happened so quickly. Irma and Karen were at the window, through which had come, first, the sounds of running footsteps on gravel and then the starting of a car. Joe, Danny and Carlos, still holding hands, had been watching the antics of the dog, wondering whether to give it any more shocks.

Carlos's hand dropped from Danny's as he stared at the closed door.

"We—we're shut in!"

The girls turned sharply. Not even the sound of a second car starting could distract them now.

"Oh, no!" cried Karen.

"Oh, *yes!*" Joe groaned.

"Well, at least we gave Gideon a head start," said Danny.

Irma nodded. She still looked grave.

"Yes," she said. "Let us just hope he makes good use of it!"

20
Buzz Goes Exploring

When the ghosts didn't check in at one o'clock, Buzz and Wacko became impatient. They were not only dying to hear the results of Buzz's call. They also had some new information of their own.

When the ghosts didn't check in by 1:30—after Wacko had made several trips to the front door—their impatience began to turn to anxiety.

"Listen!" said Buzz. "Something must have happened to them. Something connected with what your father mentioned over lunch, maybe. Tell me again. *Exactly* what he told your mom."

Wacko shrugged.

"Simply that Gideon had been reported to the police. 'That guy I found loitering outside in the car,' he said. 'Detective Grogan called to ask if we'd seen him around since. I said, "No, why?" ' Then Grogan told him that Gideon had been caught snooping around Camp Wednesday this morning, inside the director's house, but had managed to get away before he could be questioned."

"And did your dad say whether Grogan was taking it seriously?"

"Well, he must have. Like I told you before, Grogan had sent someone around to the Lakeview Hotel, and they found out that Gideon had checked out in a hurry."

They continued to wait, staring at the blank screen, with Wacko going to the door another two times.

At 2:00, Buzz was almost beside himself.

"That does it," he said. "I'm going to see if I can find out what's going on. You stay here, in case they turn up while I'm gone."

"But—where—?"

"Camp Wednesday. Where else? I'll take a ride out there on my bike. Maybe they're on their way. At least I can give Carlos a ride."

"You're not going *in* there?" said Wacko, horrified.

"Well, maybe not in the camp itself," said Buzz. "Just cruise around the outskirts, sort of."

"Well, for Pete's sake, see that you *do* keep to the outskirts!"

"Don't worry!" said Buzz. "The worst that can happen is if it starts dumping a blizzard on me!"

As he approached the camp along 106, he slowed down. The sky was a dark bruise color, but it wasn't just that. He had started to realize what a remote place that camp really was, once you'd gone down the long

146

dirt road. And to remember what had happened there, eighteen months previously. How much easier it would be *now* to dispose of a body, when the men had the place all to themselves. Or *almost* all . . .

He was passing the place haunter's house at that point. He tried to picture the fat angry lady ghost. The house seemed very quiet, with no sign of any normal life.

Then he remembered how they'd said Mr. Quigley had been taking a shortcut through there, on his way out of the camp.

"Why not?" he thought, turning into the driveway. "That's the route Joe and the others might be taking, too."

He decided first to make sure there really was nobody home. After all, *he* wasn't invisible, and that would be just perfect—getting reported for trespassing himself!

No one answered his ring at the front door. He wheeled his bike around the side, noticing that the garden there did look pretty good—falling down in terraces to the trees and the splashing of a hidden stream. That would be the stream that ran into the camp lake, he figured. That would be—

Then he stopped.

There was a car parked around the back, well out of sight of the road. He'd only seen Gideon's once before—but he recognized the rather unusual deep rust color. Glancing back at the house, he went up to the car—then grinned. Sure enough, there was a Polinsulation sticker low down on the windshield.

He went and banged on the back door of the house, just to make sure. There was still no answer. His grin broadened.

"You've got to hand it to that guy!" he murmured. "He is one cool cookie!"

And he imagined Gideon collecting his bags at the hotel, and then—instead of doing the expected and hightailing it out of the area—sneaking back and hiding the car on Mendelssohn's doorstep.

"*He* must have noticed the place looked deserted, too. Well"—Buzz looked down the garden path, twisting between rose beds—"if Gideon thinks it's safe to go in by that route, who am I to hang back? Who knows? I might be able to help him."

Ten minutes later, having left his bike in the undergrowth at the side of the stream, Buzz cautiously emerged from the trees. The lake spread before him, pewter-colored under the still-threatening sky. The statue loomed on its island, adding to the sense of menace.

Buzz licked his lips. They had become very dry.

Maybe he was too exposed. Maybe he should stick to the trees and work his way up to the rest of the camp under their cover.

He turned, and was just about to put his new plan into operation, when something crashed through the twigs behind him, snarling as it came, and knocked him flat on his face into the undergrowth.

"Keep very still!" came a voice, through the angry, rasping, panting sound. "Or the dog will tear you to pieces!"

Buzz kept very still. The dog's breath was hot on the back of his neck. Some warm sticky fluid began to trickle around the nape, and for a second he thought he'd been bitten already. But it was only the dog's saliva.

"Prinz!" said the voice—then something in German.

The weight left his back.

"You may turn around and sit up now," said the man, reverting to English. "But very slowly indeed."

Buzz didn't need to be told twice. The dog was still only a growling couple of feet from his face. The man was observing him with ice-cold eyes.

"So?" he drawled. "Who are you and what do you want?"

"I—I was only exploring," said Buzz. "I was wondering what the fishing was like, and I really didn't realize I was trespassing. Not until I saw the lake, and then I realized . . . I realized . . ."

His voice trailed off. At first it had seemed like the man believed him. He had begun an impatient nodding. But very soon the cold eyes had narrowed, and a *very* evil smile had started to curl around the tusks.

"Prinz," the man said softly, "it looks like you have caught yourself a ghost!"

Buzz started. The dog growled.

"A—a ghost, sir?"

The man gave the dog a gentle pat.

"A telephonic ghost, Prinz." Then he addressed Buzz directly. "Some people never forget a face. I—my telephonic friend—never forget a *voice!*"

Buzz's mouth fell open. He suddenly wished he'd stayed home with Wacko, after all.

"It seems you've lost that voice," said Wolfgang. "We must see what we can do to help you find it. *On your feet!*"

21
Irma's
Terrible Thought

"We have a visitor!" Wolfgang called out, in English, as they stepped inside the hall. "As no doubt you have seen already!"

The plump startled face of Mendelssohn looked up at them from the bottom of the stairs.

"No—stay with the monitors," said Wolfgang. "We'll bring him down."

Mendelssohn nodded and hurried off. Buzz felt his heart sink as he followed Wolfgang down the stairs. The dog was almost literally breathing down Buzz's neck, two steps behind.

If only he could feel a more familiar touch!

Mendelssohn was already sitting in front of the bank of television screens when Buzz was ushered in. He turned, his eyes uneasy behind the glasses.

"But Wolfgang," he said in German, "*nobody* should be brought in here!"

"Don't worry," Wolfgang said, still speaking English. "This is not just anybody. This is a ghost."

Mendelssohn stared at Buzz. He looked genuinely scared.

"A—a ghost?"

"Yes." Wolfgang prodded Buzz between the shoulder blades. "Say something—you!"

"I—I don't know what you're talking about, sir. I really, truly, don't!"

He had striven for a British accent.

Mendelssohn looked puzzled. Wolfgang smiled sourly.

"How very astute! . . . I am afraid, Dr. Mendelssohn, we have a very formidable customer here. He has the presence of mind to switch his accent. But too late. This"—he said, the smile gone—"is the person who telephoned us this morning. I was privileged a few minutes ago to hear his voice *without* any disguise."

Buzz said nothing now. If only he could feel that telltale touch!

"But no matter," said Wolfgang, affably. "So long as you use some sort of a voice, we shall all be happy. *Now!*" he snapped. "Who are you, and what are you doing here?"

"My name is Phillips. I told you—I was just exploring. Fishing."

"And the phone call?"

"I don't know anything about a phone call."

Buzz was a bad liar. He felt his face redden even as he spoke.

"Tell me," Wolfgang pursued, "what do you know about a—a person called David Rafferty?"

Buzz said nothing and looked down at his feet.

"And another person called MacGregor?"

Still with his eyes down, Buzz gave a slight shrug.

"Very well," said Wolfgang, "we shall have to *make* you speak. And speak the truth, what is more!"

Mendelssohn swiveled from the bank of screens. Twelve of them, Buzz noted, trying desperately to take his mind off what might be coming next. In four rows of three. With somewhat foggy views of various parts of the camp.

"*Now*, Wolfgang? You intend to—to interrogate him *now*? But—"

Mendelssohn gestured toward the screens.

Wolfgang sighed.

"Yes. You are quite right. You keep your eyes on the screens. Our next likely visitor will be far more discreet in his movements than this one. Prinz will take care of this one. *Prinz! Achtung!*" Buzz felt another prod. "*You* had better remain perfectly still. I shall be back shortly."

"Where—?" began Mendelssohn, casting an uneasy glance at the dog.

"I am going for something that will keep our friend out of mischief for an hour or two," Wolfgang said in English.

"And that won't be a bunch of magazines!" murmured Carlos.

The ghosts had been listening, horrified, at the door

of the next room. Their senses had been on extra alert from the moment Danny, over by the window, had spotted Wolfgang and his prisoner approaching the front door. Some words had been muffled, only the tones distinguishable. But the tones had been enough. And Wolfgang's last words had been only too clear.

"What are they going to *do?*" said Danny.

Buzz had not only been his best friend. He'd been Danny's *only* real friend, during his short lifetime.

"They'll be putting him to sleep, probably," said Joe, looking grave. "Just for an hour or two," he added, giving Danny an anxious look. "You heard what Wolfgang said."

"And *then* what?" said Danny.

Nobody spoke. Nobody dared even to look at him.

"What they did to David Rafferty?" Danny persisted. "Torture him? Then—?"

He couldn't go on.

"If only we could get word to Wacko!" Joe groaned.

"Do you think *he's* out there, too?" said Karen, her eyes widening.

"No!" said Carlos. "No chance! He'll be back home—waiting for a message. He's got more—"

Carlos broke off, with another glance at Danny. No use in going through *that* again. Telling a guy his best friend is overprecipitate, always rushing into things without thinking. Not *now!*

Danny seemed to guess what Carlos had been about to say. And to agree.

"That *would* make more sense, I guess," he mumbled. Then he slumped. "But what's the *use?* If *we* can't get out?"

In the next brief silence, Irma suddenly gasped.

Joe looked at her.

"What?"

She winced.

"I've just thought of something. About David Rafferty. It is not very pleasant." She glanced apologetically at Danny. "But—well—it is important."

"Go on," said Joe.

"Yeah," Danny grunted.

"Well, I think I know now why we've never seen his ghost."

"Why?" said Karen.

"Because—" Irma looked close to tears. "Because there never *was* one!"

"But—"

Irma's eyes, fixed on the wall between the two rooms, were burning as she continued.

"I think that David must have gone through so much torture that—somehow—in one of the lulls that beasts like these always give their victims, just to keep them alive—"

"Oh, no!" cried Karen, her hands flying to her face.

"Yes, Karen. I think that in one of those lulls, the last of them, David must have found a way to kill himself!"

The silence was so deep they could hear Mendelssohn clearing his throat softly in the next room, and the sound of a door being shut, somewhere upstairs.

They knew only too well what happened to people who committed suicide. Or what did *not* happen to them.

They never came back as ghosts. Where they went,

no one knew. But they certainly skipped the ghost stage. And—to a ghost—that was like being killed twice. In their eyes, people who deliberately drove other people to suicide were far worse than murderers.

"Let's hope that Gideon can do something," whispered Karen.

There came the sound of more doors being opened and shut upstairs.

"Against two armed men and that dog?" said Irma.

"Isn't he *ever* armed, himself?" asked Joe.

"I doubt it. I was at his briefing in Jerusalem, remember. And he was given strict instructions. Absolutely no lethal weapons in a friendly country. He is a crack shot—they all are—but he's only been allowed to use an air pistol. For very special purposes. For darts."

"Tranquilizer darts?" said Karen. "For dogs? Well, at least—"

"No," said Irma. "It isn't impossible, I suppose. But these were darts containing very small microphones. Bugs."

Carlos gasped. *Now* she'd told them! *Now* he could see—

Then he shrugged.

What use was that knowledge *now?*

But it gave him his idea.

"Look!" he said. "We can't just hang around here. We *have* to get through to Wacko. I'm going out."

"How?" said Joe, looking up sharply.

"The hard way."

156

Carlos was already striding to the window.

Danny rushed forward and clutched his arm.

"No, Carlos! Let *me!* Buzz was *my* best friend!"

Carlos gently removed Danny's hand.

"And what use do you think *you'd* be?" he asked, trying to smile. "It needs someone who can—" He glanced at Irma. "Well, Danny—think. *You* know what I can do and no one else can. So"—he turned back to the window, his brave smile wobbling badly—"here goes!"

"Oh, Carlos, *no!*" screamed Karen, realizing what he meant to do.

Joe put a hand on her shoulder.

"Just don't look, Karen. He—he'll be OK. Our job is to listen out and hope for a chance to help Buzz directly."

Carlos heard none of this. His mind was concentrated on that one-inch gap as he slowly reached up, palms down, fingers tight together. . . .

22
Carlos Does
a Mickey Mouse

It took only a few seconds for Carlos to squeeze through, but they were the worst he had ever spent in either his life or his afterlife.

He had heard that if you kept your eyes closed, it was less alarming, less totally and completely revolting.

Well, Carlos did try to keep his eyes closed, especially when his head was going through. But his scientific curiosity had gotten the better of him, and when he felt the upper part of his head had reached the other side, he opened his eyes—and nearly swooned.

It was as if he'd lost his sight completely, so narrow was his field of vision now, and so wide. It was just like a thin bright thread, stretching out forever on either side. He raised his head—the lower part was now emerging—and there was no sky. He lowered it— and there was no earth, no driveway. Just the long thin strip of blinding light.

But then—within a couple of seconds that seemed like a month—he realized he could pick out objects in that strip: a pale blue streak that was already assuming the shape of a vastly elongated Porsche, and the white corners of the house front—very far right, very far left.

That encouraged him. At least his head seemed to be returning to something *like* its normal shape. One object after another began to appear in the widening slit. He could now see the skyline—jagged over the tops of green smears that had to be fir trees—and the gray white ribbon of gravel below him.

He continued to squeeze forward. First the shoulders. Then the chest. And only when he heard a shrill piping and an almost unrecognizable voice—flattened into a deep gruffness—saying, "Cut it out, Karen! Just don't look!"—did he realize that his ears must have been affected, too.

He tried not to think of it. Already his eyes were improving. There was just a terrible choking feeling that really bothered him, and he knew—he had thought of this many times, when he'd been considering the phenomenon of Mickey Mousing—that this feeling was purely imaginary.

Sure, the ghost body did go through a flattening process. Or, if the aperture had been a small hole, a spindling process. But it wasn't like your physical body. Life couldn't be crushed out by physical pressures—whether wood or stone or steel or water. Only other ghosts could do that—by the pressure of their own bodies, their hands or feet. So—no matter how distorted a ghost's body became as a result of physical pressures—they didn't threaten the life inside. They probably didn't even affect the functions the way they *seemed* to do.

Imagination—that was all.

Plus the programming the mind had received during the body's regular lifetime.

So Carlos *hoped*. . . .

When he was completely through the crack and got to his feet, he had another jolt.

Such horribly distorted feet—flattened and splayed, twice their normal length and seemingly far, far below him!

How could he ever move about on *them?*

He felt himself sway. He shut his eyes. The swaying ceased.

Imagination, he reminded himself.

It has to be imagination.

So—walk!

Go on!

Walk!

There's Buzz in there, due for a terrible death, and you, Carlos Gomez—are you going to let that happen, just because you're feeling a supernatural kind of dizziness? An *imaginary* dizziness?

He stepped forward.

It worked.

He took another step.

That worked, too.

He opened his eyes. His feet *still* seemed remote—and treacherously narrow.

So what?

Ice skates are narrow, aren't they?

Move, man—move!

By the time he'd reached the dirt road, he was making good progress. His field of vision was still unnaturally wide, and he still felt grotesquely taller and wider. But if he didn't look down at himself, it wasn't so bad. And—well—who normally, living or ghost, continually looks down at his or her own limbs? It would be when he was closer to town, with more ghosts around, that he figured he'd have to take a tight grip on himself. Seeing the horror or disgust on their faces.

Because he knew *that*. He wouldn't be a pretty sight, even by then—even with his body getting back to normal shape.

How long would it take to get back to normal, though?

Some ghosts said no longer than half an hour. Others said hours.

He sure hoped the first bunch was right!

One thing was certain, anyway. It wouldn't be like those Saturday morning cartoons. All those Mickey Mouse–type cartoons from which the phenomenon had gotten its name. Those Tom and Jerrys, Tweety Birds, Looney Tunes, whatever. Where the cat flattened by a steamroller regained its normal shape within seconds. Where the dog's nose—pulled through a keyhole, foot after stringy foot of it—snapped back into its normal shape like elastic, as soon as the character at the other end released it.

Carlos could well understand now why the majority of ghosts could no longer bear to *look* at those scenes on the TVs of the living—let alone laugh at them. And why those who'd been through the process themselves were made positively sick by the sight. Why—

His heart gave a jump. He had reached the highway by now, and it seemed that fortune was favoring the brave *this* time, anyway.

A farm tractor was trundling in the direction of town and behind it was a small procession of crawling vehicles. Carlos didn't hesitate. He leaped onto the trunk of the nearest car.

And only just in time, too.

The tractor turned off, and the traffic surged forward. All he needed now was for the car to keep going, into the town itself, and maybe even to the section where Wacko lived. And then—

Well, *what?*

Carlos took a peek at his fingers and winced.

They were almost normal, sure. The gap hadn't been *that* narrow. But the knuckles, the hand itself, and the wrist—especially the wrist—still looked terribly misshapen. He tried to flex his fingers. They moved slowly, jerkily. He closed his eyes and tried again. Better. Much better.

Imagination, that was all!

Then he blinked.

What kind of imagination, though?

Had he been imagining they'd lost their flexibility, influenced by the look of them? Or was he imagining they had regained their flexibility, just because he *wasn't* looking at them?

162

We'll worry about that later, he told himself. Meantime, let's hope we don't get held up by any more tractors!

Just over ten minutes later, Carlos was standing in front of the word processor. To his relief, he'd found Wacko in the front yard, looking terribly anxious. He was pretending to take the air, but actually waiting for either the sight of Buzz or the touch of some other member of the Ghost Squad. Carlos had lost no time in giving him that touch, noting, with a sinking feeling, a slightly puzzled frown as Wacko had brushed his top lip immediately afterward. Had the recent flattening made a difference? The impression of a wider fly, a wider droplet of water? In which case—

So Carlos worried as he flexed his fingers over the keyboard. What if he activated the wrong keys? Or none at all?

"Come *on*, you guys!" Wacko groaned, staring at the screen. "What's keeping you?"

Carlos closed his eyes, flexed his fingers again, sighed.

Would he be able to do it? Would he be able to let Wacko know that Buzz's life was in such grave danger, and the sooner Wacko got hold of Grogan the better?

He began to stab the air above the keys.

23
Buzz Feels a Touch

At about the time that Carlos had reached the highway, Wolfgang returned to the monitoring room. He was carrying a large roll of adhesive tape, two inches wide, and a pair of scissors.

Buzz gulped. He felt his mouth going dry again.

Wolfgang smiled.

"To immobilize you with," he said, in answer to Buzz's unspoken question. "Please—your hands behind your back—*slowly!*" The dog had growled. "That is better. Now cross them at the wrists."

The man applied the tape rapidly and methodically, giving each turn—over, between, and over again—a sharp cruel tug. And when he'd finished binding the wrists together, he snipped the tape and went to work on the hands, making a kind of stiff mitten on each, with fingers and thumb jammed close together, incapable of any useful movement.

"Just in case you contemplate picking at the tape around your wrists," murmured Wolfgang, sounding like a medic whose only concern was for the patient's good.

"And now," he said, "your feet together, please. Leaving a space of about two inches. We do not want to have to carry you. . . . That's a good lad!"

Wolfgang's hobble binding was as tight and secure as that at the wrists, except that Buzz was left with enough freedom of movement to shuffle precariously, a few inches at a time. Wolfgang made him do this, watching closely as Buzz covered the trial distance to the door. On the way back, Wolfgang stepped behind him and gave him a push. It wasn't a vicious shove. Just enough to make Buzz hobble faster, totter and start to fall.

Wolfgang grabbed him by the collar and yanked him upright, in time to save him from falling flat on his unprotected face.

"Forgive me!" he said. "I wished to make sure that you were not moving more slowly than you were capable of. We are very thorough at Camp Wednesday."

"Yes, and so is—!"

Buzz cut himself short.

"And so is *whom?*" said Wolfgang, looking pleasantly surprised. "*Who* is very thorough? Besides ourselves?"

Buzz kept his mouth closed.

"Well—*who?*"

"The police," Buzz mumbled, feeling his face go red again. "When they find out I'm missing."

"Oh, the *police!* Sure! But was that *really* whom you were referring to?"

This time Buzz made no reply at all.

Wolfgang sighed and cut off a short length of tape.

"Very well. Since you express such a strong urge to remain silent—for the *time being,* of course—we will do our best to accommodate you."

As Wolfgang plastered the strip across Buzz's mouth, so firmly and fiercely that the boy felt that his lips had begun to peel and bleed already, Mendelssohn gasped.

"Wolfgang! The number five screen!"

Wolfgang turned. Buzz saw that one of the screens had gone blank. He felt a surge of hope.

"That's the camera at the rear of the cabins," murmured Wolfgang, speaking German now as he fiddled with some controls. "It *could* be a fault, I suppose."

"Yes, but—"

"I know, I know! It could also be Mishcon."

Buzz drew in a sharp breath on hearing the one word he could recognize.

Wolfgang turned.

"Take *him* into the next room," he said, irritably. "While I have another try for a picture."

Mendelssohn got to his feet, frowning.

"But Mishcon may head for that room first! The 'broken catch' you—"

"All the better!" snapped Wolfgang. "If he finds this fool in there, all trussed up, it will surprise him, break his concentration, delay him. *If* he ever gets this far. Now—hurry. This is no ordinary fault, I'm sure. And take the rest of the tape and fix him to the table leg."

"Of course. And then—?"

"Then Prinz and I will go see if we can put a stop to Mishcon while you keep watch here. With your pistol at the ready."

When Karen heard the words, "Take *him* into the next room—" she turned.

"They're bringing Buzz in here!" she said.

"When?" said Joe. "Now?"

"Soon—hush!" Karen listened hard. "Yes," she said. "It looks like Buzz is going to be some kind of extra bait for Gideon."

"He *is* around, then?" said Irma, her eyes lighting up.

"They think so—but hush, please—I—yes—they're coming *now*."

"Get ready!" said Joe.

They were all very tense.

"What do we do? Give Mendelssohn the Chain Boost?"

Joe shook his head.

"Just scaring *him* won't do much good. No . . . Are you *sure* they're coming in here, Karen?"

"Yes. They've put some kind of hobble on Buzz's legs, I think. And—"

The door opened.

Danny groaned. His friend looked in such bad shape.

Buzz's clothes were streaked with drying mud, from his fall at the edge of the woods, and his face looked strained and very pale—especially around the tape on his mouth.

Danny couldn't help rushing forward to touch Buzz's forehead. Buzz blinked, pausing in his hobbling.

"Come on, come on!" muttered Mendelssohn. "Over to the table."

Danny touched Buzz's forehead twice more. The effect was remarkable. The strain seemed to leave Buzz's face in a flash. The eyes brightened. There was even a slight jauntiness in his hobble as he obeyed his captor.

"Listen," said Joe as Mendelssohn stooped to his task of taping Buzz to one of the table legs. "Karen, Irma—I want you to stay in here with Buzz. Keep touching him. Let him know we're around. And if they do start torturing him, use the Chain Boost to try to throw them. Concentrate on Mendelssohn—he's the weak one."

"But—" Danny's eyes had gone wide with protest.

"No, Danny—you're going out there with me. We must try to help Gideon. He's the only real chance we have right now. At least we can throw a scare into the dog again."

"But with only *two* of us linked up," said Karen, "the charge might not be powerful enough."

Joe sighed.

"We'll just have to hope it *will* be. . . . Anyway—" Mendelssohn was straightening up. "Ready, Danny?"

Danny nodded, still looking doubtful.

"Do not even try to escape," Mendelssohn said to

Buzz. "You may be very lucky. If the person lurking around is who we think he is, there will be no need to question you at all."

"No," Irma whispered. "They will simply kill him."

Fortunately for Danny, he didn't hear those last words. He was already out in the corridor with Joe and Mendelssohn, and the door had been closed behind them.

24
Showdown at Camp Wednesday

Wolfgang was taking no chances, when he set out on his search with Prinz. He had drawn his pistol even before leaving the house, and, as he crossed the driveway, he held the black long-barreled weapon in a way that told Joe the man was an expert: slantwise, high on his chest, ready to be aimed and fired at the turn of his wrist.

Wolfgang paused and stooped to the dog, after they'd gone a few paces into the trees. He murmured some German words, and the dog went loping ahead, not too fast, along one of the paths. Wolfgang followed at a distance of fifty feet or so.

"Come on, Danny," said Joe. "He's relying on the dog to sniff out the intruder first. We ought to keep up with it, if we can. Ready to throw a scare into it again."

So they proceeded, on soft brown-needled paths that threaded through the trees, downhill, toward the main camp buildings—the dog first, then the ghosts, then the man. Danny kept glancing back to make sure Wolfgang was keeping up. The man was moving quietly, almost as silent as a ghost himself.

Suddenly, the dog stopped. It had reached the intersection of some wider trails. It turned and looked inquiringly at the man.

Wolfgang caught up, still with the gun at the ready and his eyes flitting from side to side.

When he reached the dog, he bent down and said something very softly—pointing to a path that continued downward to the right.

"Did he say something about cabins?" said Danny.

"I'm not sure," said Joe. "The dog seems to have understood, anyway."

The dog was moving more slowly now, stopping every few yards to sniff the air and listen, its ears pricked well up. Then suddenly it stiffened and went bounding away. That only made the man go more slowly, if anything. His eyes had gone to slits. His head was making a regular sweep—to left, to right.

"Come on!" said Joe. "Never mind *him!*"

They began to run, stopping only when they heard a bark, followed by another.

The first bark had a snarling undertone.

The second started that way, but quickly died into a strangled whine, followed by a whimper, then silence.

The ghosts ran on, into a clearing which gave glimpses of the camp buildings and the lake beyond. The dog lay on its side, as still as the gray boulder nearby.

"Is—is it dead?" Danny whispered.

Joe shook his head.

He pointed to the dog's neck. A dart with a tuft of black feathers was deeply embedded there. There was a glistening spot of purple red where it had gone in.

"Irma was right," he murmured. He looked around. "Can you see anything of Gideon?"

"No. Let's see if he's—"

Joe pulled Danny back. Wolfgang was approaching—very, very cautiously—crouching low, pausing at every bush and boulder. Danny looked puzzled.

"But—"

"The only possible way we can help Gideon is by using the Chain Boost on Wolfgang. Like if he should spot Gideon and take aim. We might—just might—be able to spoil his shot by touching him on whichever eye he lines up with his sights."

"He might not feel it—only two of us."

"No. But it's our only chance. Anyway, my guess is that Gideon's in control of the situation. Aside from not having a gun."

"How about the air pistol?"

"I doubt if he'll try using it on Wolfgang. He'd have to get too close. And even if he did plant a dart in him, it might not work quickly enough. Not on a guy with his finger on the trigger of a real gun."

Joe looked around. Wolfgang had stopped a few feet away, still crouched low. The sight of the dog lying there didn't seem to have stirred any emotion in him at all.

"Anyway," said Joe, "all this'll be going through Gideon's mind. Not to mention *his*."

Wolfgang was now lying prone, next to the dog, between it and the boulder. His eyes flitted watchfully as he fastened the top button of his shirt. Still watchful, he felt for the collar of his jacket and pulled it up as high as it would go. Then he replaced the glove on his left hand, using his teeth, without relaxing his right hand's grip on the gun.

"See that?" said Joe. "Only his gun hand and the top half of his face are exposed. Gideon would have to get *very* close to hit him with a dart now. And also be sure it didn't lose half its strength going through cloth."

"But he still won't know that Gideon doesn't have a real gun as well!"

"No. That's why he's being so cautious. Hoping to—"

Joe stopped.

Down below, a shrill warbling whistling had shattered the general silence. Wolfgang raised his head, turning it slowly, this way and that. Then he lifted himself up and went off in a crouching, hopping, scrambling run, down to the right.

"What—?"

"It's an alarm. He seems to know just where it's coming from, too. I think Gideon must have made his first big mistake. Come on!"

They found Wolfgang mainly by following the direction of the warbling—the man had gone off at such a lick. When they caught up with him, he was flattened against the wall at the side of the main entrance to the RT Labs. Gun still at the ready, he was peering through the partly open door. His face was grim, but there was a glint of satisfaction in his eyes.

A pane of glass had been shattered near the door handle. Slowly, stealthily, Wolfgang stepped into the vestibule. There must have been a concealed switch there somewhere, for when he reached up, the warbling suddenly ceased.

Then he waited, listening, alert for the first sound of a movement further inside. A smile had appeared on his face—an evil, gloating smile. Wolfgang was beginning to relish the hunt.

"Oh, gosh!" groaned Danny. "I don't like the look of this! What does Gideon think he's—?"

His voice was drowned by another squawling, warbling, shrieking. It seemed to be coming from behind them, over by the administration building.

Even Wolfgang looked startled. Then he bared his teeth in a silent snarl and went loping off in that direction.

"Hey! Hold it, Danny!" Joe was grinning. "I think I know what Gideon's strategy is. And Wolfgang is falling for it!"

"What?"

"Gideon's luring him away from the house. He's probably figured on taking Mendelssohn first. I mean, Mendelssohn's a bag of nerves—a much easier proposition for a guy without a gun. Come on! We'll certainly be able to help Gideon up *there!*"

Joe was right. Not only was Gideon crouching behind the Porsche when they reached the house, but Mendelssohn, true to form, had come rushing out in a panic. They saw him standing beyond the corner of the house, at the bend of the driveway. The trees thinned out at that point, and Mendelssohn was peering through the gaps, down toward the main buildings. He was obviously wondering why the alarms had gone off, and whether he'd better go down and join Wolfgang or stay put. The gun in his hand—the twin to Wolfgang's—hung limply by his side.

Gideon was watching him like a cat stalking a plump sparrow. And, like a cat, he seemed to be gauging the distance.

Then he turned his head sharply.

Joe and Danny heard it at the same instant.

A high thin humming sound, from one of the basement windows.

Danny groaned, but it was all right.

Mendelssohn would have been too far away to hear it anyway—and by now he'd taken a few steps farther along the driveway and was partly out of sight.

The humming was coming in shorter, weaker bursts.

Danny ran to the window.

"It's Buzz!"

Buzz was purple in the face, trying to yell through the gag. He must have heard the alarms go and the sound of Mendelssohn running out of the house. He must have decided it was worth trying to attract attention. Karen was looking anxious and touching his left ear for no. But Irma was closer to the window, and her face lit up when she saw first Danny, then Joe, then Gideon himself.

"It's all right, Karen!" she said. "Gideon's here!"

Gideon crouched, still with an eye cocked in Mendelssohn's direction. Then he turned to the window and said, in a low voice, his mouth close to the gap, "Keep quiet, please. I'll get you out."

Buzz's eyes rolled upward—but it was with relief. Gideon put his hand on the top of the window, then withdrew it.

"This may be booby-trapped," he said. "Just be patient."

Then he crept back to his post behind the car, watching the bend in the driveway. Mendelssohn's white shirt was showing through the trees. His back was to the house. Gideon darted to the edge of the trees, opposite the car. And he was just preparing to work his way toward Mendelssohn, when the glimpses of white shirt began to jump and twist, and three shots rang out, punctuating the screams that had shrilled out with the jumping.

Gideon fell flat on his face, instantly.

"No! No!" Mendelssohn was screaming. "Get away! Stop touching me! I—it was *not* I! I didn't want to kill you, David! I truly didn't!"

Then another two shots.

Gideon's eyes widened. The strain must have been too much for Mendelssohn, he thought, getting up and moving swiftly forward. Good!

"Shall we give him another touch?" said Danny, still linked with Joe, delighted with the success of their latest move. "Let him know that bullets can't stop ghosts?"

"No. Here's Gideon now. If Mendelssohn lets off another couple of shots he might get lucky and hit the only guy who can get Buzz out of there alive."

Gideon was moving slowly. The air pistol was in his hand. He took his last three steps very fast and jammed the muzzle into the back of Mendelssohn's neck.

"Keep quite still, Mueller, or I'll blow your head off!" he rasped.

Mendelssohn did as he was told—as far as his now convulsive trembling would allow.

"But—but—!"

"Shut up! Just lower that gun and let me take it from you."

Mendelssohn's fingers were limp. He made no attempt to resist. Gideon glanced at Mendelssohn's gun and thrust the air pistol back in his pocket.

"Now," he said, sounding deeply satisfied, "we will go back into the house, release the boy and wait for your right-hand man. Understand?"

"Yes—but you are making a big mistake! I—*Wolfgang!*"

Gideon had spotted Wolfgang at the same instant. Wolfgang himself had been taken by surprise as he'd emerged from the trees, closer to the Porsche. His pistol was only halfway to the mark. Gideon tightened his left arm around Mendelssohn's throat and, using the man as a shield, said, "Drop that gun, Schmidt! You're too late!"

Wolfgang froze. The gun stayed where it had been, pointing in the wrong direction, but still in his hand.

"Really?" he said.

"Yes. If you tried to use it, you would only kill your old commandant, Gruppenführer Heinrich Mueller. And I should kill you in any case."

"Please, Wolfgang, do as he says!"

Wolfgang laughed. His teeth looked venomous. He ignored his comrade.

"But, Mr. Mishcon—what are you saying? What do *I* care about the swine?"

Mendelssohn's chin jerked against Gideon's arm.

"You!" he screamed. "*You* are the swine!" He wriggled. "Mr. Mishcon, please! *He* is Heinrich Mueller, not I! *He* is the Ghoul of Grünberg! I am just—"

"Silence!" roared the other. "Remember your oath!"

His gun began to move.

Gideon stared. His momentary look of perplexity vanished. His eyes had gone very hard.

"Drop—" he began.

It must have been the sound of brakes as the police car pulled up somewhere behind him. But he didn't make the mistake of looking back. Neither did Wolfgang take his eyes off Gideon.

Only Joe and Danny, standing with linked hands next to Wolfgang, saw Detective Grogan and the two uniformed cops dive out at the far side of the car, dragging a startled Wacko with them. And, naturally, only Joe and Danny saw Carlos rising from his perch on the trunk, his grin of triumph fading.

"This is the police!" Grogan yelled. "Put down those guns or—"

His own gun had been ready cocked.

But it wasn't that that went off.

Joe had frantically prodded at Wolfgang's right eye, his other hand linked tight with Danny's. But whether the man felt it or not, it didn't make the slightest difference. He never took his eyes off Gideon's eyes until he squeezed the trigger. Then he did drop the gun as, clutching his chest, he fell sprawling on the grass at the edge of the driveway, his already sightless eyes staring up at the sky.

Gideon's own eyes were obscured by blood from the hole in his forehead. But there was a smile on his lips—the same shy smile of the young salesman he'd pretended to be.

"This one's dead," said the cop crouching at the side of Wolfgang.

"So is this one," said Grogan, easing Gideon's body to one side, to get a better look at Mendelssohn. "They must have fired simultaneously."

"Don't tell me *he's* croaked, too," said the second uniformed cop, looking down at Mendelssohn.

"Not quite," said Grogan. "Looks like a heart attack. Better call an ambulance. . . . And get that *kid* away from here!"

Wacko had been staring at the body of Gideon. He started when the cop placed a hand on his arm.

"There's Buzz!" he said. "He's in there, in the house, somewhere!"

Joe gave him a touch on the right ear. Right for yes—and now, hopefully, right for, "Don't worry. Buzz is OK. Just do what the man says, Wacko."

Wacko looked up and blinked. All around, in the trees, some birds had started to sing—strange sweet piping whistles, like someone was calling in a dog. He looked them up later. White-throated sparrows. In all his future years, he would never hear that call again— that dusk chorus—without tears coming to his eyes.

"Come on, son." The cop steered him slowly to the

car. "Better sit out here, on the bumper. You look like you could use the fresh air."

Numbly, Wacko sat down. He closed his eyes. And now he could feel more ghostly touches, brushing his face, one after another. It was as if not only Carlos and the others had come clustering around, trying to reassure him, but dozens of strange ghosts, too. Hundreds of them . . . *Thousands* of them . . .

"Snowing at last!" grunted the cop, reaching into the car for the radio handset.

Wacko nodded as he opened his eyes and saw, through the slow downward dance of the snowflakes, Detective Grogan going into the house.

25
Rumors, Reports— and Returns

Strange things happened around town during the next few weeks. Strange reports were published, and even stranger rumors began to circulate.

Most were connected with Camp Wednesday.

Three people had died there, all within an hour. One of them was the camp director himself, the much respected Dr. Mendelssohn. He'd been shot, said one report, and his servant had died of shock. A report issued shortly after the first one said no. It had been the other way around—though there *was* some doubt about the true relationship between the two men.

There was a similar conflict over the identity of the third man. A private investigator, said one report. A burglar, said another. A siding rep *mistaken* for a burglar, said yet another.

Before the local press and media could go much further, the men from the State Department arrived—carloads of them—and promptly sealed off the camp. After that, security was much tighter than in the days of the good Dr. Mendelssohn, who'd been no slouch himself, what with that stone-faced servant of his and the fierce dog.

Then came the rumors about the statue. Seems there *was* a statue there, in the middle of the lake—the rumormongers said. And—know what? Those State Department guys had gone and demolished it. Probably they were looking for a stash of money—millions of dollars the doctor had failed to report to the IRS.

Others said no—it wasn't money. It was a body. Maybe several bodies. At least *twelve*. The only person who came near the mark was a waiter at the Lakeview Hotel. A man and woman who'd signed themselves in as Mr. and Mrs. Smith of Kansas City had stayed for a couple of days—but the waiter swore their real name was Rafferty. He'd seen them the year before, when they'd stopped by for a meal after visiting the camp to make inquiries about their missing son. *Then* the woman had looked drawn but dry-eyed. This time she went away weeping, but somehow—well—relieved.

Then the word began to spread that something much bigger had happened. That the infamous war criminal Heinrich Mueller, the Ghoul of Grünberg, had finally been run to earth there. That he'd been hiding in a root cellar for over thirty years—the secret guest of Dr. Mendelssohn.

Others said no—it was Mendelssohn himself who'd been the Ghoul. But those who'd ever had dealings with his man, Wolfgang, were more inclined to agree with the third proposition: that Wolfgang himself was Mueller, and that by switching roles with his old wartime servant, he hoped to throw any would-be war-criminal catcher further off the scent.

By the time these stories had started to circulate, journalists, cameramen and commentators from all over the world had started to flock in. The Lakeview Hotel alone was booked solid for eight weeks in advance.

Detective Grogan was soon ignored by the news-hounds—much to his relief. Anyway, he'd been strictly forbidden to answer any questions, beyond reiterating his original statement that the fracas at Camp Wednesday had been blundered into by a couple of local kids, one of whom had innocently strayed into the grounds. Some reporters suspected the kids' motives had been rather less innocent. That they'd somehow been tricked by the Mysterious Mister M— as the newspapers had started calling Gideon—into helping him with his snooping.

Grogan himself was of the second opinion. When he'd asked Wacko that first afternoon how he'd come by this Ghoul of Grünberg yarn, Wacko had said, quite truthfully, "Gideon Mishcon." And when Grogan had asked how come Gideon had gone to *them* for help, Wacko had replied—again quite truthfully—that the Israeli authorities must have heard of Wacko and Buzz's earlier successes in the same area.

Maybe Grogan would have dug deeper, but quite soon the State Department had stepped in, and his time was taken up in helping their men to comb through Camp Wednesday, foot by foot.

The strange incidents and rumors not apparently connected with Camp Wednesday—or only indirectly so—got less wide attention.

Like the sudden lifting of the depression of a kid called Andy Quigley after receiving a surprise phone call. Just one call after two years of unsuccessful treatment by troops of psychiatrists and therapists. It seemed like a miracle.

Like the sale of a house on 106 to a keen garden-loving couple who couldn't believe their luck—reputedly at a heavy loss to the owners, who'd been hoping to sell it for twice the amount.

Like the ribbing received by a local police-dog handler when he claimed he could retrain a fully grown Doberman that seemed to have developed a bad anxiety state, especially when it felt a sudden draft. Impossible, said the scoffers. And so it seemed—until the cop had a brain wave, took a crash course in German at his own expense and started issuing his commands in that language. "Prince"—it transpired—was now responding marvelously, though was still slightly puzzled when he received words of praise.

Perhaps the strangest incident of all was one that took place outside the town's livery garage only a couple of days after the shooting. Strange because it was completely invisible to the driver of the airport limo and the passengers assembling for the afternoon run to Kennedy Airport.

"Are you *quite* sure you don't want to stay awhile longer?" said Karen.

Irma smiled.

"I'd love to. But no. I must go back. As long as my sister continues to work as a flight attendant, I must watch and listen. Terrorists never let up, you know."

Joe nodded.

"Well, at least you know where to come if you want to get a warning through to the living."

"There isn't always time, I'm afraid!" said Irma. "But thanks. I know how much your secret means to you." She turned, with a smile. "Are you *sure* you couldn't teach me your methods, Carlos?"

(She still didn't know about the word processor. Only that Carlos had some kind of special telepathic rapport with Wacko.)

Carlos grinned bashfully.

"I'm sorry. I—I don't really know how I do it myself. And—well—it's just something I can use with Wacko. And no other ghost could do it—not even these guys."

"You can say that again!" muttered Danny.

Karen looked embarrassed. She'd come to like Irma very much. But Joe was right. The fewer ghosts who knew the secret, the better.

She changed the subject.

"Are you feeling better now? About Gideon?"

The tears started in Irma's eyes. But she smiled, and nodded.

"I guess so. It seemed such a shock, such a waste! Even though he did succeed in what he'd set out to do. But—you're right. Gideon will be coming back. He is just the type."

"Yeah," said Joe. "Another three or four months, and there'll be a new face in the Israeli ghost community. Then—"

He broke off—suddenly grimacing.

"What is wrong?" asked Irma.

"I just thought of something. There'll very likely be a new face in the ghost community *here*, before long! The Malev variety!"

That thought stunned them all. Mueller/Wolfgang—whatever one called him—had been a tough and terrible adversary as a living person. But as a *Malev*—

Karen shuddered.

"I—I think the driver's getting in," she said.

The man had just tossed his half-smoked cigarette straight through her. It was sizzling on a heap of snow at the side.

Irma got in while the door was open and took a spare seat. And, as they waved her out of sight, Carlos said, "Well, let's get back to Wacko and Buzz. I promised to tell them where that bug was planted. Not that it matters now, of course."

"Right!" said Danny. "So where *is* it? Why don't you even tell *us?*"

"Because he has a great big head and likes to show off!" said Karen.

"Not all *that* big, I hope!" said Carlos, smiling ruefully, thinking of his recent ordeal.

Then, laughing and chatting, they went back to Wacko's, stepping lightly and printless over a new layer of freshly fallen snow.